Raves for

UNDEAD AND UNWED

"What can you say about a vampire whose loyalty can be bought by designer shoes? Can we say, outrageous? . . . A hilarious book."

—*The Best Reviews*

"*Undead and Unwed* is an irreverently hilarious, superbly entertaining novel of love, lust, and designer shoes. Betsy Taylor is an unrepentant fiend—about shoes. She is shallow, vain, and immensely entertaining. Her journey from life to death, or the undead, is so amusing I found myself laughing out loud while reading. Between her human friends, vampire allies, and her undead enemies, her first week as the newly undead is never boring . . . A reading experience that will leave you laughing and 'dying' for more from the talented pen of MaryJanice Davidson."

—*Romance Reviews Today*

"A hilarious book." —*Paranormal Romance*

"This book is fantastic. These vampires are different from any that I've read about . . . The lead characters are strong and independent, the action fast and furious . . . This is one of the most erotic books that I've read in years." —*Escape to Romance*

Titles by MaryJanice Davidson

UNDEAD AND UNWED
UNDEAD AND UNEMPLOYED

Undead and Unemployed

MaryJanice Davidson

BERKLEY SENSATION, NEW YORK

UNDEAD AND UNEMPLOYED

A Berkley Sensation Book / published by arrangement with the author

PRINTING HISTORY
Berkley Sensation edition / August 2004

Cover illustration by Chris Long.
Cover design by Joni Friedman.
Interior text design by Kristin del Rosario.

For information address: The Berkley Publishing Group,
a division of Penguin Group (USA) Inc.,
375 Hudson Street, New York, New York 10014.

ISBN: 0-425-19748-4

BERKLEY SENSATION™
Berkley Sensation Books are published by
The Berkley Publishing Group,
a division of Penguin Group (USA) Inc.,
375 Hudson Street, New York, New York 10014.
BERKLEY SENSATION and the "B" design
are trademarks belonging to Penguin Group (USA) Inc.

PRINTED IN THE UNITED STATES OF AMERICA

10 9 8 7 6 5 4

For my former bosses: Jim, Linda, Bob, Vince, Maggie, Neil, Kathy, Pat, Jeff, and Ron. Some of you were terrific, some of you I suspected were sociopaths, but all of you taught me something.

Acknowledgments

As always, this book would have been more difficult without the help of my husband, Anthony, who keeps the kids out of my hair when I'm on deadline, reads everything I write, and thinks I'm gorgeous. He's right, of course, but I appreciate the reminder. He also comes up with the "Undead" titles and believe me, some of them are a real scream.

Thanks also to my family, who are staunchly supportive and, I swear, get more excited over these book deals than I do.

Thanks also to Cindy Hwang, whose edits usually include "More Sinclair!". Fans of the vampire king have her to thank.

And special thanks to the Magic Widows, my book club and dear friends, who listen tirelessly to my book ideas and plots for taking over the world.

And the first who shall noe the Queen as a husband noes his Wyfe shall be the Queen's Consort and shall rule at her side for a thousand yeares.

—THE BOOK OF THE DEAD

If that rat bastard Sinclair thinks I'm going to be his wife for a thousand years, he's out of his fucking mind.

—FROM THE PRIVATE PAPERS OF HER MAJESTY, QUEEN ELIZABETH I, EMPRESS OF THE UNDEAD, RIGHTFUL RULER OF THE VAMPIRES, CONSORT OF ERIC I, LAWFUL KING

Prologue

Police interview of Robert Harris.
June 30, 2004
55121 @ 02:32:55–03:45:32 A.M.
Filed by Detective Nicholas J. Berry
Fourth Precinct, Minneapolis, Minnesota

AFTER being treated at the scene, Mr. Harris denied the offer of hospital care, and consented to accompany the responding officers, Whritnour and Watkins, to the precinct for an interview.

The interview was conducted by Minneapolis Detective Nicholas J. Berry.

Robert Harris is a fifty-two-year-old Caucasian male who works for Bright Yellow Cab as a taxi driver. Mr. Harris was on duty during the events transcribed below. Mr. Harris has passed a breathalyzer; labs are pending on possible drug use.

DETECTIVE BERRY: Are we ready? Is the tape . . . okay. Would you like something to drink? Coffee? Before we start?

ROBERT HARRIS: No thanks. If I have coffee this late, it'll keep me up. Plus, y'know, with my prostate, it's just asking for trouble.

DB: Can we discuss the events of this evening?

RH: Sure. You wanna talk about the Twins getting their asses kicked, or why I was dumb enough to take a job where I haveta sit all the time? Goddamned hemorrhoids.

DB: The events—

RH: Sure, you wanna know what I meant by that story I told those fellows, the ones who took care of me. Nice enough fellows, for a coupla flatfeet. I don't mean no disrespect by that, either. I mean, that's why we're here, right?

DB: Right.

RH: Because you guys think I'm crazy or drunk.

DB: We know you're not drunk, Mr. Harris. Now, earlier this evening—

RH: Earlier this evening I was sittin' on my ass, thinking about my kid. She's nineteen, goes to the U.

DB: The University of Minnesota, Duluth Campus.

RH: Yup. Anyway, that's why I pull so many second shifts, because cripes, those books are expensive. I mean, a hunnerd and ten bucks for a book? One book?

DB: Mr. Harris—

RH: Anyways, so there I was, mindin' my own business, eating my lunch. Course it wasn't exactly lunchtime, cuz it was ten o'clock at night, but when you're on second shift, you do what you can. I was sittin' at Lake and 4th. A lot of the cabbies don't like that neighborhood, you know, because of all the Negroes. No offense. I mean, not that you look it, but—

DB: Mr. Harris, I'm not African American, but even if I were, I'm sure I would devoutly wish we could stay on course.

RH: But you never know these days, am I right? Goddamned P.C. Nazis. A man can't speak his mind anymore. I got a friend, Danny Pohl, and he's just as black as the ace of spades, and he calls himself a-well, I'm not going to tell you what he says, but he uses it all the time. And if he don't care, why should we?

DB: Mr. Harris . . .

RH: Sorry. Anyway, so I'm in this neighborhood, which, yeah, some people say ain't so great, and I'm eating my lunch—ham and Swiss with mustard on Wonder Bread, in case anybody needs to know—when all of a sudden my cab was on its side!

DB: You didn't hear anything?

RH: Son, I didn't have a single hint. One second I was eating, and the next I was lying on my side and all the garbage on the floor was raining down on me and I'd dropped my sandwich and the side of my head was resting on the street. I could hear somebody walking away, but I couldn't see nothing. But that wasn't the worst of it.

DB: What was?

RH: Well, I was still trying to figure out what happened, and wonderin' if I could get the mustard out of my new workshirt, when I heard this really loud scream.

DB: Was it a man or a woman?

RH: Tell you what, it was hard to tell. I mean, I know now, because I saw them—both of them—but I didn't know then. Whoever was yelling was having their legs pulled off or something, because they were shrieking and crying and babbling and it was the worst sound I ever heard in my life. And my daughter's tone deaf and is always takin' up new musical instruments. Like that time with the tuba. But that was nothing compared to this.

DB: What did you do then?

RH: Well, shit, I climbed out of the passenger side of my cab as fast as I could, what d'ya think? I was a medic in the war—Vietnam, that was. I hung it up after I got back stateside and I never went to a hospital again, nope, not even when my wife, God rest her, had Anna. But I figured I could maybe help. My cab was insured, I didn't mind about that, but someone was really in trouble and that was a lot more important. I thought maybe somebody had backed over their kid by accident. Some of those alleys are pretty dark. Hard to see stuff.

DB: And then?

RH: Then the bus pulled up. It almost hit my cab! And that was weird, because it was pretty late for the buses to be running, and this one was empty except for one passenger.

Then this gal jumps out. And the bus just sits there. I seen the bus driver just staring at the gal like she was made of chocolate ice cream. And then I got a good look at her.

DB: Can you describe her?

RH: Well, she was tall, real tall—'bout my height, and I'm just shy of six feet. She had light blond hair with them streaky—what d'you call 'ems? Highlights! She had kind of reddish highlights, and the biggest, prettiest green eyes you'd ever seen. Her eyes were the color of them old-fashioned glass bottles, those real dark green ones. And she was real pale, like she worked in an office all the time. Me, my left arm gets brown as a berry in the summertime, on account of how it's always hanging out my cab window, but my right arm stays real white. Anyway, I don't really remember what she was wearing—I was mostly looking at her face. And . . . and . . .

DB: Are you all right?

RH: It's just this part's hard, is all. I mean, this gal was maybe five or six years older than my daughter, but I—well, let's say I wanted her the way a man wants his wife on a Saturday night, if you know what I mean. And I'd never been one to horndog after kids young enough to be *my* kid, and never mind that my wife's been dead for six years. So it was kind of embarrassing, too, that even though those awful screams were still sort of echoing in the air, here's me all of a sudden thinking with my dick.

DB: Well, sometimes, under stress, a person—

RH: Wasn't stress. I just wanted her, is all. Like I never wanted anybody. Anyways, I stared at her but she didn't pay me no notice. Gal like her, she probably gets old coots like me staring at her twenty times a day. She didn't say nothing to me, just marched back toward the alley. So I followed her. There was a couple of street lights back there, so I was finally startin' to be able to see stuff. Made me feel a lot better, I can tell you.

And just like that, before we could even get there, the screams stop. It was like someone had shut off a radio, that's how sudden it was. So the gal, she starts to run. Which was funny to see, because she was wearing these teetery high heels. Purple, with bows on the backs. She had teeny feet, and these pretty little shoes. It was kind of funny to see that.

DB: And then?

RH: Well, she could sure move in them shoes, and that was a fact. She musta been a real track star or something. And I was right behind her. And we get to the alley, and right away I seen it was a dead end, and I didn't want to go too far in. It's funny, I never think about the Nam no more, but that night it was like I'd just gotten back home. Man, I was noticing *everything*. I was really wired.

DB: Could you see anyone in the alley?

RH: Not at first. But then the gal says, real loud but firm, you know, like a teacher, "Let him go." And then I seen there were two guys and they weren't standing ten feet away! Don't know how I missed them before. One of them was this little short squirt, but he was hoisting a guy bigger than me, holding him up off the ground! He was slamming the guy into the brick wall real hard, and the big guy's head was sort of lolling all over the place, and he was out cold.

But then, when the gal talked, the little guy let go, and the guy who'd been doing all the screaming hit the bricks like a sack of sand—I mean, he was *out*. And the little guy marches up to us, and all of a sudden I was just scared shitless.

DB: Did you see a weapon, or—

RH: Nothin' like that. He was just . . . bad, I guess. He was about a head shorter than me and he had kind of gray skin. And one of those little black mustaches, real thin. Me, I think a man should grow a real soup strainer or nothing at all.

Anyway, he looked like a little punk, but there was somethin' about him—I just wanted to get away from him. It was like somethin' inside me knew he was bad, even if I couldn't see for myself exactly what it was. And let me tell you, I watched my own dear wife die from cancer of the stomach. She went an inch at a time and it took eight months. I didn't think nothing would ever scare me after watching that. But that guy . . .

DB: Do you need a break, Mr. Harris?

RH: Hell, no, I wanna get this over with. I promised I'd come down and tell you, so here I am. Anyway, this guy, he gets real close, and he says, "This is none of yours, false queen." And the way he talked—it was real old-fashioned. Like, I dunno, like people talked maybe a hundred years ago. And his voice—Jesus! I got goose bumps all over. I wanted to run, but I couldn't move.

But the gal didn't seem to care. She straightens right up and says, "Oh, blow me. Get lost, before I lose my temper."

DB: "Blow me"?

RH: Sorry, but that's what she said. I remember it real well, because it was a shocker. I mean, I'm a big guy, and *I* was scared. She was a kid, and she didn't sound scared at all.

DB: Then what happened?

RH: Well, the little mean guy, he looked like he was gonna fall over. I was shocked, but he was . . . well, he was *really* shocked. Like no one had ever talked to him that way in his whole life. I dunno, maybe no one had. And he says, "My meals are none of your business, false queen."

That's what he kept calling her—"false queen." Never did hear her name.

DB: "False queen."

RH: Yeah. And she says, "Sit and spin, jerk off." Seriously! Then she says, "You know as well as me that you don't have to scare 'em or hurt 'em to feed, so cut the shit." Or maybe it was "cut the crap." Anyways, she was ticked off.

DB: And then?

RH: Then he grabs her! And his lips peeled back from his teeth, like a dog getting ready to bite. *Just* like that, our neighbor's dog Rascal went rabid last summer, and before I shot the poor dog, he looked just as crazed and out of control as this guy.

And before I could help her—I was scared, but I didn't want her to get messed up, I mean, I woulda done *something*—she whips out this cross and jams it onto his forehead! Just like in the movies! And man oh man, I thought the *big* guy was a screamer. This guy, he yowled like his lungs had caught fire, and all this smoke starts pourin' off his forehead, and oh, Lord, the smell. You wouldn't *believe* how bad it smelled. Like pork on fire, only the pork had been spoiled first. God, I'd like to puke just thinkin' about it.

And he let go of her and kind of staggered backward, and she steps up just as cool as a cucumber and says, "You'll pick this gentleman up and you'll take him to the hospital. And you'll pay for the bill if he doesn't have insurance. And if I catch you feeding like this ever again, I'll shove this cross right down your throat. Got it, or should I get out the hand puppets?"

And he sort of cringes away from her and nods. She was so stern and beautiful, he couldn't look at her. Shit, *I* could hardly look at her! And then he picked up the big guy, who was still conked out, and sort of ran out of the alley with him.

Then the gal turns to me and kind of sighs, like she's real tired. Then she says, "Did you ever get stuck in a job you really hate?" And I allowed as to how that had happened to me once in a while. Boy oh boy, she was somethin' gorgeous.

DB: And then?

RH: Then she asks am I all right. And I say I am. And she says for me not to be scared. And I say as long as she's there, I won't be. And she gave me a big smile for that one.

So we started walking out of the alley, and she sees my cab laying on its side. And she looks all disgusted and says, "Jeez, what an infant." I guess she meant the guy who ran away. And she walks over—this is the part you're interested in—and kneels down, and slips two fingers underneath my cab, and lifts it back up until its on its wheels again.

DB: She lifted your cab upright?

RH: Yup.

DB: With one hand.

RH: With two fingers. I know how it sounds. It's okay. The other cops didn't believe me, either.

DB: And then what happened?

RH: Then she looks at me with those pretty green eyes—except now they were more hazel then green, which was kinda strange, I dunno, maybe her contacts fell out—and says, "I think it'll still run. Sorry about your trouble." And I tell her it's okay. And she climbs on the bus—which was still waiting for her by the way, which could be the weirdest thing that happened tonight—and waves good-bye to me. And then the bus drove away. Ran down a mailbox and through a red light, too.

DB: That's it?

RH: Ain't that enough? It was some night. Tell you what, that gal was something else. I don't *never* want her mad at me.

DB: Because of her strength?

RH: No. Because I wanted her, but I was scared of her, too. I'm just glad she turned out to be nice. Because what if she was like that little guy in the alley? The vampire?

DB: You believe the man was a vampire?

RH: Shit, who else would scream and be burned by a cross? What I'd like to know is what *she* was.

DB: You believe in vampires, do you?

RH: You've been a good listener, son, and I appreciate it, but I want you to pay close attention to just one more thing. I was in a war when I was just a teenager. And I found out that the guy who don't believe his eyes is the guy who goes home in a bag. So, yeah. I believe in vampires.

Now, I mean.

END INTERVIEW

03:45:32 A.M.

Chapter 1

WHEN I'd been dead for about three months, I decided it was past time to get a job.

I couldn't go back to my old one, of course. For one thing, I'd been laid off the day I died, and for another, they all still thought I was six feet under. Plus, a job during daylight hours just wasn't going to work anymore.

I wasn't starving or homeless, at least. My best friend, Jessica, owned my house and wouldn't let me pay rent, and she had her team of super accountants pay the other bills despite my strenuous objections. I sure didn't need to grocery shop for much except teabags and milk and stuff. Plus, my car was paid off. So my monthly expenses were actually pretty low. Even so, I couldn't live off Jessica's charity forever.

So here I was, on the steps of the Minnesota

Re-Employment Center. They had evening hours every Thursday—thank goodness!

I walked through the doors, shivering as I was greeted by a blast of air-conditioning. Another thing about being dead that nobody warned me about was that I was cold pretty much all the time. Minneapolis was having a severe heat wave, and I was the only one not hating it.

"Hi," I said to the receptionist. She was wearing a stiff gray suit and needed her roots done. I couldn't see her shoes, which was probably just as well. "I came to the unemployment center to—"

"I'm sorry, miss, that's RE-Employment. Unemployment centers are an anachronism. We're a responsive twenty-first-century re-employment one-stop center."

"Right. Um, anyway, I'm here to see one of the counselors."

For my audacity, I spent the next twenty minutes filling out paperwork. Finally, my name was called, and I was sitting in front of a counselor.

He was a pleasant-looking older fellow with dark hair, a gray-flecked beard, and chocolate brown eyes, and I was relieved to see the wedding ring as well as the photo of his pretty wife and *de rigeur* adorable kids. I fervently hoped he had a happy marriage, so he wouldn't make a fool of himself once my undead charisma smacked him in the face.

"Hi, I'm Dan Mitchell." We shook hands, and I saw his eyebrows go up in surprise when he clasped my clammy palm. "Elizabeth Taylor, right?"

"That's me."

"Are your eyes all right?"

I was wearing my sunglasses for two reasons. One, the fluorescent light hurt like a bitch. Two, men didn't fall under my spell if they couldn't see my eyes. The last thing I needed was a slobbering state employee humping my leg.

"I was at the eye doctor's earlier," I lied. "He put those drop things in."

"Yeah, been there. Elizabeth Taylor—just like the movie star!" he enthused, obviously having no idea people had been drawing that conclusion since the day I'd been born.

"Betsy."

"Betsy, then." He was flipping through the reams of paperwork I'd handed him. "Everything looks right . . ."

"I hope so. I'm here for Unemployment—"

"We're the RE-Employment Center," Mitchell said absently, still flipping.

"Right, right. Anyway, I need a new job, and while I'm looking, I'd like Unemployment Insurance. In fact, I have a quest—"

Mitchell looked vaguely alarmed. "Um . . . I need to stop you right there. We can't do that here."

I blinked. Not that he could tell behind the Foster Grants I was wearing. "Come again?"

"We're a re-employment office. That's what we do."

"Sure, okay, I get it, but don't you . . .?"

"If you want unemployment benefits, you need

to call the hotline. Or use the Internet. I'm sorry, but we can't answer your question here."

"Let me get this straight. This is the place I go to when I'm unemployed . . ."

"Yes . . ."

"And you have unemployment benefit applications here—"

"Absolutely!"

"But you don't have any staff here who can help me get unemployment benefits."

"Yes, that's correct."

"Oh, okay." This was weird, but I could be cooperative. Probably. I leaned back in the uncomfortable plastic chair. "Okay, so, can I use your phone to call one of these hotlines?"

Mitchell spread his hands apologetically. "Ah, jeez, you know, we used to let people do that, but some folks abused the phones, and so—"

"So you're telling me I can't call an Unemployment Hotline using a telephone in the Unemployment Office?"

"Well, technically, remember, we're not an Unemployment Office anymore"—I suddenly wondered if a vampire could get drunk. I decided to find out as soon as I got out of this bureaucratic hellhole—"and that's why we can't let you do that." He shrugged. "Sorry."

I whipped off my sunglasses and leaned forward, spearing him with my sinister undead gaze. It was a rotten thing to do, but I was desperate. "I need. To use. Your phone."

"No!" He hunched over and clutched the phone protectively to his chest. "It's against policy!"

Amazing. I was sure my vampire mojo would leave him putty in my hands, but apparently his bureaucratic training was stronger than ancient evil.

"You'll just have to go home and contact them on your own dime," he snapped.

I stomped back to the waiting area. Outrageous! I wasn't just any undead tart, I was the queen of the vampires!

"Don't forget to fill out a customer satisfaction survey on your way out!" Mitchell yelled after me.

God, kill me now. Again, I mean.

Chapter 2

THE flashing red lights in my rearview mirror produced their usual result: a surge of adrenaline, then annoyance. I hadn't been going *that* fast. And it wasn't even a patrol car pulling me over. It was a Chrysler, for God's sake.

One of the many people dedicated to ruining my day got out of the car and started toward me. He didn't have that slow, arrogant strut that staties have. In fact, he was jogging. I recognized him at once and groaned.

Nick Berry. Detective Nick Berry, to be exact, and absolutely the last person I wanted to see. We had an embarrassing episode last spring, and I lived in fear that, one of these days, he'd remember I was dead. Or at least, remember he'd been at my funeral.

He slipped into the passenger seat. "Hey, Betsy. How's it going?"

"You're abusing your authority as a sworn officer of the law," I informed him. "I wasn't even barely speeding."

"Yeah, yeah. Listen, where were you the other night?"

"Which one?"

"Saturday?"

Uh-oh. "Home," I said, putting plenty of fake curiosity in my tone. "Why?"

"I don't suppose anybody could back you up on that one?"

I shook my head. "Marc was at the hospital, and Jessica was probably at home—I didn't see her that night. Why? What's going on?"

Nick leaned back, easing his feet through the garbage on my passenger side floor. He didn't know how lucky he was. It had been a lot worse when I'd been eating solid food. "Cripes, don't you ever clean out your car? How many shakes do you drink in a week?"

"None of your business. Now go away and catch bad guys."

"I'm going to need a tetanus shot when I get out of here," he complained, kicking an empty 7-Up cup off the end of his boot.

"Seriously, Nick, what's up? I mean, if you're not giving me a ticket—"

He shook his head. "It's stupid."

"Well, I figured."

"No, really stupid." While he babbled, I let my gaze roam over his blond hair, his swimmer's build, his chiseled features—then jerked my gaze back to the road where it belonged. That's how we'd gotten into trouble the last time. I'd been newly undead and unbelievably thirsty, he'd been handy, I'd drank his blood, and he'd been lost. For a long time. Sinclair had to step in and fix it. I still had no idea what—if anything—Nick remembered.

". . . and this nutty old cab driver described you. I mean, not that there aren't about a zillion blondes in Minneapolis, but still. The description fit you pretty well. It was the shoe thing, actually, that caught my—"

"Well, obviously it wasn't me," I lied. "Doy."

"Doy? Haven't heard *that* in about fifteen years. But anyway, I think you might be right. The whole story was just . . . I think the guy was . . . I don't know. Maybe some of it was real, and some of it he imagined, or made up to get attention. He seemed like a lonely guy." Nick was rubbing his temples in a way that made me distinctly nervous. "I . . . sometimes I have dreams and they *seem* real . . ."

"That happens to everybody." Should I zap him with my vamp mojo? Would it interfere with whatever Sinclair had done, or would it make things better? "Maybe you need a vacation."

"That was a funny thing that happened to you last spring," he said, changing the subject. At least, he *thought* he was changing the subject. "I mean, not everybody has a mix-up like you do."

"I still say it was my stepmother playing a joke. It's not like she wouldn't want to see me dead."

"Yeah, but going to the extent of a fake funeral—or was there a funeral?" He was rubbing his temples so hard, they were getting pink. "I dreamed about it, but mostly I . . . I . . ."

"Nick, for crying out loud!" I said loudly, hoping to snap him out of it. "I've got stuff to do. So are you going to get out of here or what?"

His hands fell to his lap at once, and he seemed to shake off the trance-like state he'd fallen in. "So sorry, Betsy," he said sarcastically. "What, there's a shoe sale somewhere?"

"As a matter of fact, there is. Look, I hope you catch the bad guy—"

"Yeah, yeah, I'm sure you're on pins and needles. Never mind. Saw your car and couldn't resist. But, I gotta get back to it."

"Okay. Nice to see you again."

"You, too. Stay out of trouble." He smiled at me and climbed out of the car, unaware of the straw sticking to his heel. "Have a good one."

"Bye!" I called, and waited until he pulled out in front of me before I got my car moving. It was just as well; I was shaking like a leaf. Poor Nick was crawling all over the truth, and didn't have a clue. I wished I could confide in him, but enough people knew my dirty little undead secret as it was.

Besides, once I *had* confided in him. And it had been an utter disaster. I wasn't making the same mistake twice.

* * *

AN hour later I was at the finest, most glorious place on the planet: The Mall of America. Or, if you're a shopper, Heaven on Earth.

I decided to trudge through the first level of Macy's to cheer myself up, and then drown my sorrows in two or ten daiquiris on the fourth floor.

Like any great idea, the Mall (never "the mall") is something familiar, made bigger. A lot bigger. Everyone has parked in a lot and walked into a store. Here you had to walk a long, long time to get to the store, is all. It helped to memorize the state you were parked in. You know how most parking lots can name their sections after two or three animals? "Oh, honey, don't forget we parked in the marmoset lot." The Mall was so big, they couldn't use animals. Animals are puny. They used states. And not little states like Rhode Island, but big honking states like California and Texas.

I parked in Texas and crossed the small side street to Macy's. As always, I was struck by the beauty of the building. The red brick and soaring windows reminded me of—don't laugh—a church. And the star they used instead of the apostrophe in Macy's seemed so heavenly.

Once inside, I inhaled the sweet smell of perfume, leather, cotton, and floor cleaner. Before I'd been laid off I was a secretary. Now I was jobless, unless you counted the whole queen of the vampires gig, which I certainly did not, not least because it didn't pay for shit. Besides, most days I doubted I was the queen. Certainly the other vampires I'd been crossing paths with lately didn't think so. And Sinclair . . . Never mind about Sinclair. I wasn't going to think about that jerk.

I zoomed in on the shoe department like a blonde homing pigeon. Shoes, shoes everywhere! Ah, sweet shoes. I truly think you can take the measure of a civilization by looking at its footwear.

Because I was in a department store, I was enveloped in its time warp. So although the fourth of July was less than a week away, the shoe department had all their fall colors and styles on display. That was all right. I already had twenty-two pairs of sandals.

I eyed the row of Kenneth Cole boots, finally taking down a vibrant red pair and feeling the leather. They'd look terrific with my black duster, but I already had a pair of red boots. Hmm . . . should that make a difference?

I also checked out the Burn footwear. They were supposedly all made by hand—and for two hundred dollars a pair, they'd better be—but I'd never tried a pair. Maybe when I got a job, I'd treat myself, give them a try.

Typical of Macy's, the saleswomen were all ignoring me because I wasn't waving fifty dollar bills at them. I tapped the nearest one on the shoulder. "Excuse me, could I see the new Etienne Aigners?"

She looked at me over the tops of her black cat's eye glasses. A much too harsh a color for her face, by the way. They made her pale skin look even paler, and her brown eyes kind of muddy. "I'm sorry, miss, we don't have any."

"Oh, sure you do. I understand if you haven't had time to go through them and put them on display, but I'd just like to see them."

I could see another saleswoman and a balding man in a gorgeous Armani suit watching us from a distance. He was holding a clipboard and wearing a Macy's name tag. The woman beside him was staring at her coworker, who'd obviously woken up that morning with a need to be unhelpful.

"We really don't have any—"

"Who do you think you're talking to?" I asked impatiently. "The Aigners have been out for six days. You probably got them four days ago. I just want to see if he put out a lavender pump like he was supposed to."

"Listen, you—"

"Brigid."

The saleswoman cut herself off and looked over at the guy who'd been watching. I'd heard them coming, but she hadn't, because she jumped and looked terribly guilty. "Yes, Mr. Mason?"

"Please come to my office. I need to talk to you. And Renee"—he turned to the other saleswoman—"please take our customer in the back and show her the Aigners."

"Ha! I mean, thanks."

"This way, miss," Renee said, smiling. She was shorter than me by a good four inches, with brown hair and red highlights, and hazel eyes that looked at the world through classic wire rims. She had lots of freckles and natural, high color. She was wearing a red-and-black plaid suit, black tights, and Nine West black flats. Pretty, in a "brainy girl who grew up to be classy" kind of way.

She walked me through a door in the back of the shoe section and then let loose with a stream of giggles. "Holy cow! You really told Brigid. She's toast. She was supposed to have that display up the day before yesterday."

"Don't ever get between me and a new line of shoes," I said. "Others have found that out to their sorrow. I guess I should follow that up with an evil laugh, because it sounds sort of ominous."

Renee snorted and escorted me past the discount racks. The Aigners were scattered all over the floor, mixed in with Nine West's crap from last season.

"Oh, the humanity!" I gasped when I saw the mess.

"*Big* trouble," Renee muttered.

"Help me straighten this out!"

"Uh . . . okay. I mean, you don't have to. They're just shoes."

I swayed on my feet, and didn't trust myself to reply. Instead, I got to work, and Renee helped.

Within ten minutes, we had all the Aigners lined up like dead soldiers, close to the door. They were a little dusty, but no major damage. The Nine Wests I'd kicked into the far corner. Alas, no lavender pumps.

Just as well; I couldn't afford to buy shoes today, anyway.

"That's better," I said, dusting off my hands. I heard the door open behind us but, since Renee didn't react, I didn't turn. Jeez, how in the heck did I get along before, without vampire hearing? "It won't take long to get these to the floor."

"You know a lot about shoes," Renee said, staring. "I didn't even notice the Jude pumps had gotten mixed in with the others, and I've been here four months."

I tried not to shudder at her ignorance; it wouldn't be nice. Luckily, the dude rescued me. "Excuse me, ladies. Find everything you needed?"

"Unfortunately, no. Maybe he'll do it next season."

"Mmmm." His name tag read John Mason, Store Manager. He looked like my dad's accountant . . . balding, glasses, good suit, great shoes. He smelled like Calvin Klein's One and baked potatoes. "We are now short a sales associate for the shoe floor," he announced. Renee pursed her red lips in a silent whistle and rolled her eyes at me, where Mason couldn't see. "Are you by any chance looking for work?"

I stared. John Mason, Store Manager, was a genius or a telepath. "Yes, I am! What a coincidence, I mean, that you would ask me!"

"Not really." He pointed to my purse, where the paperwork I'd gotten from the Re-Employment Center was sticking out. "Would you like to work here?

Not on commission," he added sternly. "I can pay you nine dollars an hour."

"Wh—sure! When can I start?"

"I'll need you here every evening, Wednesday through Saturday," he warned.

"You bet! I can only work nights, anyway."

"Well, then."

Before I could kiss him on the mouth, Mr. Mason had walked me over to Human Resources and gotten me my paperwork. I was a little worried at first—I had died three months ago, after all. Would my social security number work?

It did. Thank you, government backlog!

The paperwork finished, Mr. Mason handed me my name tag and bid me good night.

Betsy Taylor, it said.

Macy's, it said.

BetsyTaylorMacy's. Wow. Oh, just . . . wow. Really totally wow.

Outside the store, I did a little skip step of joy . . . and nearly sailed over a car by mistake. I probably could have pulled that off even if I hadn't been dead.

Wow! Me, working for Macy's! That was like a fox working for a chicken farm. It just didn't get any better.

Chapter 3

I hurried home to Apple Valley to tell Jessica all about my new job. But the unbelievable stench assailed me on my front step, and I almost couldn't make myself go inside.

I fidgeted on the front step for a minute, debating, and finally told myself, well, you defeated the most evil vampire on the planet just a couple of months ago, so you can do this, too.

I opened my front door and followed my nose to the bathroom, where my best friend was lurched over the toilet.

"Still have the flu?" I asked sympathetically.

"No stupid questions from vampires," she groaned. She retched again. I observed she'd had chicken soup and toast for lunch. "Use your super strength to pull my head off my shoulders, please."

"For crying out loud, Jess, how long you been in here?"

"What day is it?"

I noticed that she hadn't had time to turn on the bathroom light in her headlong gallop, and had initially missed the toilet. Oh, well. The wall needed re-painting, anyway.

When she was finished scatter-puking, I picked her up like a big doll and carried her to the guest bed. Before I'd become a vampire, there was no way I could have done this. Jessica was a few inches shorter than me, and about as pudgy as a stop sign, but she was gangly and hard to move around. Now, of course, it was cake.

I brought her a glass of 7-Up and a wet washcloth. She cleaned herself up as best she could, and then I picked her up and ran back into the bathroom so she could throw up the soda.

"Maybe it's time to go to a hospital," I said nervously. She'd been barfing for two days.

"Marc can give me a shot when he gets home," she said. She sounded hollow, because her head was all the way inside the toilet bowl. Luckily, she'd gotten her hair cut last week.

Marc was my roommate, a resident at the Children's Hospital in Minneapolis. He'd moved in the week I woke up dead. Jessica had a gorgeous, chic little seven-room place in Edina, but she spent most of her time at my place.

"Is there a reason you're being sick here," I asked, "instead of at your place?"

"You don't know how lucky you are," she replied, ignoring my question, "being dead and all."

"Right now I agree with you. Hey, guess what? I got a job."

"That's nice." She looked up at me. Her brown eyes were sunken. She'd looked better on the day of her parents' funeral. "Why are you just standing there? Why aren't you killing me?"

"Er, sorry." I took a breath through my mouth. Luckily I only had to do that about twice an hour. "You know, this sort of reminds me of your twenty-first birthday. Remember?"

"The night is"—she *hurped-hurped* for a second, then continued—"a blur."

"Well, you were mixing crème de menthe with vermouth, and then you started with Jack Daniels and tequila. I tried to get you to slow down, and you told me to shut up and get you a Zima with a bourbon chaser. Then—"

"Stop!"

"Sorry." Yeah, not the brightest move. But that was the last time she'd been this sick. "If you were a guy, or gay, I could hypnotize you into passing out. I guess I could try hitting you over the head with something . . ."

"Just help me back to bed, dead girl."

I did. I was ready to *hurp-hurp* myself, and wanted to go back to Macy's in the worst way.

Instead, I tucked Jessica back in—she dozed off while I was pulling the blankets up to her chin—and left her to start cleaning.

I found some clothespins in the kitchen junk drawer. Don't ask me why—I didn't have a clothesline. Junk drawers are a miracle in themselves. The stuff that turns up in them—why were there coupons for free bird seed? I didn't have a bird.

I found with the clothespin over my nose, and Playtex rubber gloves on my hands, and by thinking about the spring line of Ferragamos, I could scrub the bathroom without yarking up the blood I'd drank about three hours ago. My donor had been an amiable car thief who'd been fumbling with the steering column of a Pontiac Firebird when I found him. After I'd taken what I needed, I called him a cab. It was bad enough I was a lamprey on legs; I wasn't going to be an accessory to grand larceny.

I was rinsing the mop in the toilet when I heard a knock. I hurried to the living room and opened the door before Jessica could wake up.

Tina stood there, looking all big-eyed and hopeful. She took one look at my ensemble and slapped a hand over her mouth to stifle the giggles.

"Get lost," I suggested. I still wasn't speaking to her. Thanks to her, and Sinclair, I was the queen of the undead. A small fact they'd hidden until after Sinclair and I had made love. There could be no forgiveness!

"Please can't I come in, Majesty?" she asked, lips twitching madly.

"No. And don't call me that." Still, I stood there with the door open. I'd liked Tina the moment I met her. Of course, whenever someone saves my life on first acquaintance, I tend to feel warm toward them.

And except for her unwavering loyalty to Sinclair, which made her do the most annoying things (see above: the whole queen of the vampires thing), she was pretty cool. Old—something like a hundred and some years—but cool. She didn't act or talk like an old lady, though she could be stiff sometimes. And she looked like a *Glamour* cover girl with her long blond hair, high cheekbones, and pansy eyes, so dark and enormous they seemed to take up half her face.

"What on earth are you doing? And what is that stench?"

"Cleaning up," I replied nasally. I plucked the clothespin off my nose. "Jessica's got the flu."

"I'm sorry to hear that. The flu. I haven't had that in . . ." Her eyes tipped up in thought. "Hmm . . ."

"Fascinating. Look, the bathroom smells like someone died in there. I'm not exaggerating—I would know, right? We both would. So, I have to get back."

"Let me do it," she suggested.

"Forget it," I said, startled. Yech! A job I wouldn't wish on my worst enemy. Or Sinclair.

"Such work is beneath you."

"I'll be the judge of what's beneath me, missy," I snapped. "And as it happens, cleaning up puke is right up my alley."

"I insist, Majesty."

"Too bad. Besides, you can't come in without my permission. Ha! And again I say, ha."

She raised her eyebrows at me, dark and delicate as butterfly feelers, and stepped over the threshold.

"Well, nuts."

"Sorry. Old wives' tale. Besides, Eric and I were in and out of here a couple of times this past spring, remember?"

"I've been doing my best to forget all about last spring." I handed her the clothespin.

"Besides, if you think about it, it makes no sense," she said gently. "Why wouldn't a vampire be able to come and go as she pleased?"

"Spare me the lecture. And if you're going to barge in, make yourself useful. You want to clean? Be my guest."

She moved forward so eagerly, I actually felt bad for a few seconds. She was so desperate to get back in my good graces.

Not my problem.

"So, what d'you want? Why'd you come over?"

"To beg your forgiveness again," she replied soberly.

"Scrub first," I advised. "Then beg."

TINA made about as much noise as a ninja, but Jessica sat up anyway when we walked into the bedroom. "Whu?" she asked muzzily. "Tina? That you?"

"Poor Jessica!" Tina hurried to the side of the bed. Her delicate nostrils flared once, and then she was smooth-faced and polite. "If memory serves, the flu is dreadful." She put a hand on Jessica's forehead. "You must feel awful."

"I do, but that feels great," Jessica groaned. "Your clammy dead hand is just the ticket. How come Betsy let you in? Thought she was still ticked off at you and King Gorgeous."

"Do *not* call him that," I muttered.

"She took pity on me. Go to sleep, darling," she soothed. "When you wake, you'll feel much better."

Just like that, Jessica's eyes rolled up and she was out, snoring blissfully.

"Damn!" I was impressed in spite of myself. Tina was bisexual; I figured that's why she had power over men *and* women. "Nice work! I didn't know you could cure the flu."

"Thank you. Scrub brush?"

"Next to the toilet. But seriously, this is just too sad. You must have more important things to do than clean my bathroom," I commented, following her to said bathroom. "It's almost the weekend, for God's sake."

Tina flinched at "God". Vampires were so touchy about organized religion. "Actually, I did have some news."

"Sinclair has turned into a pile of ash?" I asked hopefully.

"Ah . . . no. But it's funny you should say that. We're getting reports of quite a few staked vampires."

"So?"

She looked at me.

"Ah, no," I whined. "What, this is *my* problem?"

"You're the queen."

"Oh, so I have to protect the city's vampires?"

"The world's vampires, actually," she said gently.

Good thing I was standing near the tub, because all of a sudden, I needed a place to sit down.

Chapter 4

"So, somebody's been running around killing vampires?"

"Yes. More than one somebody, most likely. We suspect a hit team."

" 'We' being you and Sinclair."

"Yes."

I drank the rest of my tea and got up to fix a fresh cup. The bathroom sparkled like something out of a toilet bowl cleaner commercial; Tina could scrub like a fiend. Did fiends scrub, I wondered idly. Note to self: find out.

"Look, Tina, no offense, but I'm not sure this is necessarily a bad thing."

"No offense taken," she said dryly.

"I just don't think it's my job to protect the city vampires, is all. Shit, I've been protecting the city from *them*. What is it about upright wood ticks that they have to hurt their food? Huh?"

She stared at her cup and didn't answer.

"I mean, just the other day, I'm minding my own business, when I have to pull a bloodsucker off his lunch. Not only did he rough up his meal, but he tipped over a city cab and scared the shit out of the driver just for the hell of it. Just because he could."

Still, Tina said nothing. I knew her blood donors were one hundred percent willing, but it was still embarrassing to be associated with the bad guys.

I jumped into the silence. "So, I'm betting this hit squad or whatever has a legitimate beef with the undead. Right? Right. Now *I* have to get involved? What the hell for?"

Tina was silent for a long moment, then finally said, "You're young."

"Oh, sure, throw that in my face again."

But she had a point. Four months ago, I'd been a live nobody. Now I was a dead monarch. But I still remembered what it was like to breathe and eat and run around outside in the daytime. Would I have cared *then* that someone was killing vampires?

Nope.

To be perfectly honest, most vampires were assholes. I couldn't begin to guess how many people I'd saved from being munched, all because vamps had victim issues. It was like, once they rose from the dead, they spent the rest of the time getting even for being murdered.

"I imagine you feel . . . torn," Tina said.

"More like annoyed and pissed off."

"But the fact remains, someone is killing your people."

I didn't say anything. Sadly, Tina didn't take the hint. Instead, she continued, "We need to put a stop to it at once."

I sat down across from her with my fresh cup of tea. "Oh, man," I sighed. "Look, let me think about it, okay? I just got a new job, my roommate's sick, my dad's scared of me, my car needs an oil change, we probably have termites, Jessica's house-hunting behind my back, and it's almost the weekend. I'm just so busy right now."

"You have a job?"

"Uh-hum." I tried to look modest. Not everybody could land the job of a lifetime. "Selling shoes at Macy's."

Another long pause. "You'll be working at a mall?"

Tina wasn't as fawning or floored as I expected. Weird. "Not *a* mall, *the* Mall, and yeah, so my plate's kind of full right now. Plus, I have to work tomorrow. At Macy's. At *the* Mall. So maybe we could pick this up later?"

She drummed her fingers on the table and stared at me. "I suppose I could get together all the information we have and bring it over later for you to look at."

"Oh, just sum up. Write me a memo."

"A memo."

"Yup." I stared at my wrist. Forgot to put on my

watch again, darnit. "My, my, look at the time! This has been great, but I've got to scoot."

"You're as subtle as a brick to the forehead. I'll be back."

"That's just swell. An undead Terminator, just what I need in my life. Give Sinclair a nice kick in the balls for me."

She sniffed. "No need to be rude."

Of course, she was dead wrong. Where Sinclair was concerned, there were all kinds of need.

Chapter 5

Four Days Later

"UM, Mr. Mason, d'you have a minute?"

We were back in the employee section, and I was standing just outside the boss's cubicle. Tastefully upholstered in blah gray, there wasn't a single picture, kid's drawing, party invitation, or softball sign-up sheet tacked to any of the cube walls. Except for a computer, his work space was clear. The place was as Spartan as a monk's cell. It was impressive and creepy at the same time. "If you're busy, I could—"

"I am, Betsy, but I'm glad you came back here . . . I need to speak with you." He took off his glasses—was it, like, a rule that if you were in management you wore glasses?—gestured for me to sit, and then polished the frames on his sweater which, weirdly, was tucked into his slacks. "But first, what can I do for you?"

"Uh, well, my paycheck seemed a little light. Not that it wasn't a kick to have a check from Macy's, because it was. But still . . . I was expecting a bit more. I was thinking maybe you guys didn't have all my hours on there, or something."

He held out his hand, and I gave him my pay stub. He scanned it once, then handed it back. "Well, there's fica, federal tax, state tax . . ."

"Right."

"And your employee discount."

"Right. What?" Damn! I'd bought a few things to celebrate my new job, but I had no idea I'd spent four-fifths of my paycheck before I even got it. Damn you, indigo blue high heels from Liz Claiborne!

"Oh," I said, sounding just so intelligent, I was sure. "I forgot about that. Sorry to bother you."

"A moment, please, Betsy. How do you like being on the Macy's team?"

"Are you kidding? It's great! It's like a dream come true!"

"I'm glad. And with one or two small exceptions, it's a pleasure to have you working here."

"Uh-oh," I said dolefully.

He smiled. "First let me say your knowledge of fine footwear is unparalleled by anyone in the store, excepting myself."

I modestly brushed my bangs out of my face. *Excepting myself, my ass. But be nice.* "Thanks."

"However . . ."

"Oh, here we go."

"I've noticed you try to talk a . . . a certain type of customer . . . out of their purchases."

I didn't say anything to that, and fought the urge to squirm in my chair. The fact was, if someone came in wearing shoes that were terribly beat up, I was loathe to sell them one of my finely made babies. Who knew what could happen? Once the shoes were out of the stores, they were beyond my protective sphere. I had to look out for my leather charges!

"Well," I finally said, "I don't like to be one of those pushy sales types."

"That is admirable, but nor should you be one of those sales types who doesn't sell shoes. Keep it in mind, please."

"Okay," I said humbly. For a minute I toyed with the idea of hypnotizing him into letting me sell to whomever the hell I wanted, then rejected the plan. I never liked forcing people to my evil will and only did it in emergencies . . . like when I was starving, or needed to cut in line at the movies.

I vowed I'd sell to the next person who asked me for help. No matter how ratty her sneakers, no matter how tatty her heels, no matter if her eye shadow had creases at the lids and her lip liner didn't match her lipstick, I'd sell her something fabulous and keep a smile on my face at the same time, even if I needed to rush into the employees' lounge and throw up afterward.

I marched back out onto the sales floor, my gaze darting about for a likely customer. Ah! There was one, and she was actually pretty well-dressed—linen jacket and navy slacks. Good shoes—Manolos, circa 2001. She was about my mom's age, and was looking at the Beverly Feldman boots.

"Hi," I said brightly. She jumped and nearly fell into the display. I grabbed her elbow and steadied her—a little too firmly. Her feet actually left the floor for a moment. "Whoa, there. I didn't mean to startle you."

She turned to look at me, her eyes so wide I could see the whites all the way around her pupils. I heard her heartbeat suddenly pick up a double-time pace, and felt real, real bad. "Don't *do* that, dear! I didn't even hear you come up behind me!"

"I'm sorry." *Nice work, Betsy, you retard. You've gone from refusing to sell to your customers to scaring the shit out of them. Stupid undead quiet feet.* "I didn't mean to scare you."

She was peering up at me. "Why are you wearing sunglasses?"

"I have weak eyes," I lied. "The fluorescents really kill. Uh . . . I just wanted to know if you had any questions."

"*I* have a question."

All the hair on my arms stood straight up and I nearly shuddered. I knew that voice. Eric Sinclair, bad-ass vampire and all-around sneak. And my consort, God help me. How's this for ludicrous: most of the vampires think I'm their queen, and that Eric's their king. *My* king.

I straightened up and stared off in the distance,

cocking my head attentively. "Yes, Satan?" I turned slowly, and faked a big smile for Sinclair. "Oops! Sorry, Sinclair. I got you mixed up with someone else."

He was standing by the tree of shoes I'd made out of Liberty ankle boots, arms folded across his chest, mouth a slash of disapproval. As always when I saw him, my undead heart went pitter. A true irony: I'd had to die to meet someone truly spectacular, and it turned out I couldn't stand him.

He was dressed in black linen slacks, a dark blue shirt, and loafers without socks. He was wearing a black suede jacket that looked like a Kenneth Cole.

As always, his charisma was like a rough wave. I had to actively resist the urge to cross the six feet between us and put my hands in his jacket, ostensibly to check the label. He was still the best-looking guy I'd ever seen, all rangy height and powerful build and black hair, and the blackest eyes. The eyes, in fact, of a devil.

Not to mention the devil's mouth. The man could kiss, and that was a fact. It was one of the more infuriating things about him. He'd never asked to kiss me. Not once. Just took what he liked. I hated him, and I hated myself for wanting him.

"I simply didn't believe it."

"What? I wasn't paying attention."

The moment had probably seemed longer than it was. I hadn't seen him since the night we had killed our common enemy, Nostro, and, er, coupled. What can I say, it had been a weird week.

I turned back to my customer, who was staring openmouthed at Sinclair. Her breathing had all but stopped. Her heartbeat was still galloping away. I gave her a poke. "We have several lovely boots in that style."

"I was certain Tina had been mistaken."

"Or I could go get some more from the back."

"So I came down to this capitalist hellhole to see for myself."

I turned. "Do you mind? I'm—*aagghh!*" He'd crossed the distance between us with his usual spooky speed, and when I'd turned I'd nearly run into his chest.

"This is intolerable."

"Pal, you don't know the half of it," I said to the buttons on his shirt. I put my hands on his broad chest—ooooh, mama!—and shoved him back a step. "Get lost, I'm working."

"My queen," he said, glaring down at me, "does not work."

"This one does," I said shortly. "And do you hear yourself? Jeez, I knew you were an ancient motherfucker, but even you must know women can have jobs now. And dammit! You made me say 'motherfucker' at work."

"No consort of mine is going to peddle footwear for minimum wage," he snapped. "Get your things right now. You're coming back to my-our-home, which you should have done three months ago."

"What home? Last I looked, your mansion was a pile of ash." I ignored the stab of guilt. Sinclair's thirty-room haven had been torched the night I got snatched by the bad guys and practically beheaded. Then I killed the bad guy and boinked Sinclair. Like I said. Crazy week. "There's no way you rebuilt it in three months."

"True," he admitted. "I'm keeping a suite at the Marquette for Tina and the others."

"Vampires are staying at the Marquette Hotel?"

"The concierge service is excellent," he said defensively. "And your place is at my side. Not in this monument to consumer greed, waiting on . . . on *tourists*."

"What are you, the Fred Flintstone of vampires? Clearly we've never met, or you forgot everything you knew about me." I clasped his hand and shook it like a Republican, which I was. His hand was cool, and twice as big as mine. "Hi, I'm Betsy. I'm a feminist, I work for my money, and I don't take orders from long-toothed jerk offs. Nice to meet you."

He had a familiar expression on his face—anger warring with a smile. "Elizabeth . . ."

I controlled a shiver. Nobody said my name like he did. First of all, nobody called me Elizabeth. And nobody did it with such a rich, rolling tone, either. He said my name the way diabetics talked about hot fudge sundaes. It was flattering, and distracting beyond belief.

I'd been shaking his hand, but now he was gripping it in both of his. This was nerve-racking, to put it mildly. I could pick up a car, and had. Sinclair was at least twice as strong. "Elizabeth, be reasonable."

"Not in my job description. Go away."

"You succeeded admirably, you know. I've come to you. You've won. Now return with me and"—he leaned in closer. His black eyes filled my world—"we'll discuss things."

I tried to pull my hand away, with no luck. I resisted the urge to brace my foot on his knee and kick free.

"I had all the discussions with you I care to have had," I squeaked firmly, hoping I didn't sound as rattled as I was. Have I mentioned that on top of everything else, Sinclair was really good at discussing things? You could say those one-on-one naked chats were his specialty. "You tricked me and you used me and you suck. Literally. And my getting this job doesn't have a damned thing to do with you, you conceited twerp."

"Then why are you here?" he asked, honestly puzzled.

The man was impossible. "Because I have to work, idiot! I have bills to pay."

He let go of my hand and straightened. This was both a relief—he wasn't looming over me like a gorgeous Bela Lugosi—and a disappointment. "I have money," he said, trying a smile. It looked ghastly, because I knew he was forcing himself not to throw me over his shoulder and head for the fire exit.

"Goody for you. It's not mine, you know. Nothing of yours is mine."

"Such lies."

"Will you stop it? Now get lost, I have two hours to go on my shift."

"I command you to resign your post."

I burst out laughing. I actually had to lean against him to keep from falling down. It was like leaning against a great-smelling boulder. Finally I wiped my eyes and said, "Thanks, I needed that. Long day."

"I was serious," he said stonily.

"So was I! Now get lost, you sneaky creep. Go find some other bimbo to lie to."

"I never lied to you."

"Why, you're lying right now! Ooooh, you've got nerve coming out your *ass*. You—"

"Ahhh . . . Betsy? Is there a problem?"

We both turned. Sinclair let out a small, exasperated growl at the interruption. As if he didn't have enough odious qualities, he was unbelievably arrogant and felt strongly that peons should keep their distance.

My boss, Mr. Mason, was standing by the cash register. He was holding one of his clipboards—he had at least five, each with a different color pen attached to the clasp by a color-coordinated string—and looked icy cool, as usual. I didn't think the man could sweat.

"There's no problem, Mr. Mason. This"—Asshole. Degenerate. Devil. Plague on my life. Lawful consort—"fella was just leaving."

Mason coughed into his fist. "Do you need a break in the green room?"

"Green room" was the code for "do you want me to get Security down here to kick his ass out, righteous?" This showed Mr. Mason was a man of high intelligence. Humans got the creeps around run-of-the-mill vamps. Something about us just set their radar off. Sinclair wasn't run of the mill. Women wanted him, and men were scared shitless of him. Deep down in their brains, they knew exactly what he was. But the women—and a disturbing number of men—ignored the part of their brain that told them to get away and stay away. Mason wasn't doing that.

"No, no," I said hastily. God knew what Sinclair would do to the rent-a-cops. "Really, everything's fine. My . . . uh . . . friend was just leaving."

"This is your supervisor?" Sinclair asked, barely glancing at Mason.

"Ind-may your own usiness-bay. Bye!"

Sinclair locked gazes with Mr. Mason. "Fire her."

Mason's eyes went blank and shiny, and he actually swayed before Sinclair. He was like a bird being hypnotized by a cobra!

I kicked the rat fink right in the ankle, bruising the hell out of my foot. "Don't you dare!"

"Betsy . . . so sorry . . ." Mason slurred, "Cutbacks . . . budget . . . exemplary performance . . . really quite knowledgeable . . . but . . . but . . . regret . . . regret . . ." He was so distressed at being forced to do something against his natural instincts, I expected him to say "Does not compute!" and start sputtering smoke.

"Go back to your cube and forget this ever happened!" I snapped. I whipped off my glasses—Macy's was divine, but the lights were fierce—and let the full force of my undead mojo, which was considerable, if I do say so myself, flare out. "Do it now!"

Mason ran out. He did it stiffly, his arms never moved from his sides. I watched him go, appalled, and then rounded on Sinclair.

"If you ever—*ever!*—do that again, I will kick your ass severe."

"Do tell."

"I mean it! Don't be coming into my workplace and making me say 'motherfucker' and hypnotizing my boss. *Now get lost!*" I could feel my face trying mightily to get red. Since my blood flowed sluggishly at best, all that happened was that I got a headache.

"You'll need my help again."

I made throwing up noises in response.

"Oh, I think so," he said coolly, but his eyes were glittering in a way I didn't like. And where were *his* sunglasses? "Your very nature assures it. As always, I am at your service. But . . ." He rested a finger on my nose. I jerked away. "There will be a penalty to be paid."

"Yeah? Will I have to listen to you whining about prophecies and concierge service? Because if that's the penalty, I'd rather eat glass than take your help."

"Agreed." He gripped my arms and lifted me up until we were eye level. This was startling, to say the least. My heart was probably pounding at ten beats a minute! I heard a double *clack!* as my shoes fell off my feet. "Before I go . . ."

He leaned in. I leaned back. It wasn't easy, since my feet were a good eight inches off the floor. "You put your face on mine, I'll bite your lips off."

He shrugged. "They'll grow back."

"Yuck! Put me down."

He sighed and set me down. "Until you need me, then." He turned around and walked out of the shoe department.

I yelled after him, "Don't hold your breath, loser!" Although he certainly could. For hours.

Strong words. But it took me an hour to stop shaking. It hadn't been easy, pulling back from that kiss.

Plus, believe it or not, I really hate confrontations.

I turned back to help my customer, but she was long gone. In fact, the entire shoe department was empty except for me. Great.

Damn you, Sinclair.

Chapter 6

"IT'S official," Marc announced. "We've got termites."

"Jeez, let me take my shoes off, willya?" I tossed my keys on the hall table and kicked off my heels. "Good morning to you, too."

"Sorry. I got the report this afternoon while you were snoozing, but I had to leave for the hospital before I could talk to you about it."

I followed him into the kitchen. He was wearing his scrubs, and had probably only beaten me home by about half an hour. He was letting his hair grow out, I noticed. It wasn't quite so brutally short. And he was gaining weight, thank goodness.

When I first met Dr. Marc Spangler, he was on a ledge ready to splatter himself all over Seventh Avenue. I talked him down and bullied him into moving in with me. He decided that living with a vampire was a small improvement over some cop scooping him up in a bucket.

He had my tea all set up for me. I'd never had a roommate before, and I sure liked it. It was really convenient living with someone who could answer the phone during the day while I was sleeping the unholy sleep of the undead. And it worked for Marc, too. I refused to charge rent, so he paid the utilities and ran my errands when he was off-shift. I had always figured doctors made more money than secretaries. I was wrong.

"Termites, huh?" He tried to show me an odious yellow paper, but I waved it away and sat down at the table. "I didn't think people got termites anymore. I thought that was, like, a '50s thing."

"Actually, they cause more damage than all other natural disasters combined."

"Somebody's been spending too much time on the Web again."

"I didn't feel like downloading more porn." He grinned, which made his green eyes sparkle. That, along with the goatee, made him look like a friendly demon.

That was probably why I liked him from the start. I only knew two people who had green eyes, true green eyes, not the lame hazel color like I had. One of them was my mom.

"Get rid of the bugs, but the house is wrecked. It's gonna cost big bucks to repair."

"Well, shit."

"Right."

"There must be something we can—did you bat your pretty eyes at the bug guy?"

"Like Scarlett O'Hara. Believe me, it was my pleasure . . . the guy was *built*. But alas, he was mostly immune to my charms. Wouldn't budge on the quote, or the bad news. Got a date Saturday, though."

"Are we sure they're termites? I thought those little bugs flying around were ants."

"Nope. *Insecta Termitidae*. In other words, we be fucked."

I sipped my tea and drummed my fingers on the table. Maybe it was time for a change, and God had visited upon me *Insecta*-whatever to get the message across.

"Maybe Jessica—"

"Shhhh!" I hissed.

"Maybe Jessica what?" the lady said, walking into the kitchen.

"Forget it," I said. "What, did I miss a memo? Are we having a meeting?"

"Actually, yeah." She yawned and grabbed the bread, then dropped two slices into the toaster. She was wearing her usual workday uniform—blue jeans, a T-shirt, and sandals. Her coarse black hair was skinned so tightly back from her skull, her eyebrows were forced up in a look of perpetual surprise. "Pretty inconvenient, too. I hate setting my alarm for two A.M."

"Cry me a river. You don't think I miss feeling the sun on my face once in a while?"

"Oh, bitch, bitch, bitch," she replied good-naturedly.

"We got the report, and it's like your guy thought," Marc said.

"Wait a minute. 'Your guy'?"

"Jess paid for the exterminator consult," Marc explained.

I let my head drop into my hands. "Marc, we can't depend on Jessica to bail us out every time we have money problems."

"We can't?"

"Marc!"

"Yeah, but . . ." He shrugged. "She doesn't care. She's got more money than she could spend in thirty lifetimes. So why should we care if she wants to help us out? It's not like she'll miss it."

"Uh, guys? I'm right here. In the room."

"Well, she's not paying to fix the house," I declared, wiping tea off my chin, "and that's that."

"Well, what do you want to do? We can't sell the house until the termites are kaput. I guess we could get an apartment . . ."

"Or a suite at the Minneapolis Marquette," I muttered. The smell of sweetly toasting bread was making me nuts. Item Number 267 that sucked about being a vampire: food still smelled great, but one bite and I'd puke. I was strictly a liquid diet girl now.

"What was that?" Jess asked, fishing her toast out of the toaster, juggling them over to the table, and sitting down.

"Guess who came to work tonight to order me to quit and move into the Marquette with him?"

"Eric Sinclair?" They said this in identical, dreamy tones. My best friend and my roommate had a severe crush. Then Jessica giggled. "Eric came to Macy's? Did he burst into flames the moment he passed the first cash register?"

"I wish. He tried to hypnotize my boss into firing me."

"Did you kill him?" Marc asked.

"I wish. Then I had to work overtime, and then I had to . . . well, never mind . . ."

"Suck blood from a would-be mugger?"

"Would-be rapist, but never *mind,* I said. I swear, the bad guys in this city are such idiots. When they see me throw their buddy ten feet, why do they assume I can't do the same thing to them? Anyway. Then I came home to the termite report."

"It's probably just as well," Jessica said with a mouthful of toast. I shook crumbs out of my eyes as she continued, "It's not like you were in love with this house. Maybe it's time for some new digs."

I didn't say anything, but I gave it some thought. I'd had the house for years . . . since I flunked out of college. My dad consoled me with a check for twenty thousand dollars, and I used it to put a hefty down payment on my little three-bedroom cottage. I'd outgrown the place years ago, but was too lazy to go through the work of selling and upgrading.

"I've got some thoughts about that," she

continued, taking a swallow of my tea. "You own the house free and clear, right?"

"You know I do," I replied, exasperated. "You're the one who paid off the mortgage when I died."

"Right, slipped my mind."

"Sure it did."

"Well, I vote we get my bug fella to spray. Then we list the house for pretty cheap. In this economy, in this suburb—"

"Oh, here goes your anti-Apple Valley rant."

"I'm sorry, I just think towns without a personality are lame," she said with the full snobbery of a twenty-nine-year-old billionaire. "It doesn't even have a real downtown. It exists because of Minneapolis. Bo-ring."

"Snot." I *liked* Apple Valley. If I wanted to go to the grocery store and the movie theater and get a hair cut and have a pancake breakfast and grab the latest J. D. Robb, I could do it all within the same half mile . . . and most of it in the same strip mall. "Big-city snot."

She tipped her fingers at me—the nails were painted lime green, I noticed with a shudder—in a mock salute. "Anyway, I figure we could get one-fifty for it, easy. Even with termite damage. And we turn around and use it to put a down payment on something more fitting for our needs."

"*Our* needs?"

"I'm getting rid of my apartment. Marc and I talked about it, and we agreed I should move in, too."

"Did I miss another memo?"

"No, just a meeting. We had it during the daytime."

"I wish you'd stop doing that," I grumbled. I thought about protesting, but Jess was over here so often, she'd practically moved in, anyway. I figured I knew why, too. My death had really shaken her up. She didn't like letting me out of her sight anymore.

And what did I care? The more the merrier. Ever since I found out monsters really do exist, I hadn't been crazy about coming home to an empty house.

"So we're agreed? We'll fumigate, list the house, and find something a little bigger. Don't worry about a thing, Bets. Marc and I will house-hunt during the day."

I drank my tea.

"Bets?"

"What, you want my approval? I'm just the figurehead."

"Well, that's true."

"But you're sure cute," Marc teased. "Even if your Macy's name tag is upside down."

A few nights later, I woke up to a world of sky blue. I had a moment of total confusion—had I fallen asleep outside? Then I realized Marc had written a note on a Post-It and stuck it to my forehead while I slept. Bastard.

Supervamp: We accepted the offer on the house, and Jessica's found us a new place. Meet us at 607 Summit Ave, 10:00 P.M. to check out the new digs.

Oh, Lord, what did she do? I crumpled the note in my fist. Summit Avenue? I did *not* like the sound of that.

I looked around my room. There were six empty boxes stacked neatly in the corner. An unsubtle hint to pack.

I showered, changed clothes, and brushed my teeth. I had no idea if other vampires still brushed their teeth, and I didn't care. Think of the morning breath of someone who drank blood for supper! I flossed, too. And used mouthwash, although the sharp medicine-mint smell was enough to make me gag.

I was getting ready to walk out the door (after tripping over the boxes in the living room), when I heard a tentative tap and opened it to see Tina standing on the step.

"Thank you *so* much for siccing Sinclair on me," I said by way of greeting. "He came to my work!"

"He did?" she asked innocently. She was dressed like a crime-about-to-happen in a red pleated miniskirt, short-sleeved white sweater, black tights, and black flats with silver buckles. Her light blond hair was caught back from her face with a red headband. She looked about sixteen years old. "Now that I think about it . . ." She pursed her red lips thoughtfully. "He mentioned he might go to the mall to see you."

"Nice try, but I'm not buying it. He doesn't take a dump without running it by you first."

"Actually, it's been several decades since either of us had to—"

"You look really cute, by the way." She was sly, but she had great taste in clothes.

She smiled, then shrugged. "I have to go out later."

"Do not tell me." Tina had a trio of devoted blood donors, but occasionally she liked to get something different off the menu. "I absolutely don't want to hear it."

"I won't. Also, here is your memo." She handed me a thick manila envelope.

"This feels like a lot of pages," I said suspiciously, weighing the stiff packet in my hand.

"I summed it up as best I could. There are photographs as well."

"Well, I'll read it when I—"

"Tina?"

"Yaagghh!" I dropped the envelope. It hit the floor with a flat thump. A second head had appeared around the door—another blond cutie—but I hadn't heard a thing. It was pretty hard to sneak up on me. Nobody alive could do it, but old vampires could.

"I'm so sorry," the cutie said. Her eyes were big. "I beg your pardon, your Majesty. I did not mean to startle you."

"Don't call me that. And you didn't startle me, you scared the shit out of me. How old are you?"

This wouldn't be very nice under normal

circumstances, but vampires loved to show off how decrepit they were.

This one was no different. She straightened proudly, and good posture did wonderful things for her. She was tall—almost as tall as me, and a good head taller than Tina—with shoulder-length hair so blond it was really almost silver, and eyes as blue as the sky on Easter Sunday. She was pale, of course, but on her it looked good. Her coloring was so fair, it demanded pale skin. She was wearing khaki shorts, a dark pink shirt buttoned at the throat, and leather sandals. She smiled tentatively.

"I'm seventy-eight, Majesty."

"Riiiiight. Well, you don't look a day over twenty-two. And don't call me that. Who are you?"

"This is Monique Silver," Tina said quickly. "She came to pay her respects to Nostro, and found a new regime in charge. There's another vampire in town, but"—Tina glanced over her shoulder—"she wouldn't come in. In fact, she's walking back to the hotel."

"She's shy," Monique said helpfully.

Tina snorted, but didn't elaborate. "Anyway, Monique's staying with us at the Marquette."

I smiled, but I didn't like that one bit. Tina staying with Sinclair was no big deal. They were practically brother and sister, and Tina didn't swing that way anyway. But I didn't care for the idea of this *Penthouse* centerfold sharing a bathroom with Eric Sinclair.

"Nice to meet you. Hope you weren't fond of ole

Notso." I said this with some anxiety—what if she had been?

Her warm smile put me at ease. "Indeed, no. In fact, I'm grateful to you. We all are . . . Betsy?" Her eyebrows—so pale and fine they were almost invisible, which made her face look like a sexy egg—arched.

"Betsy," I said firmly. "No Majesty. Thank God you catch on quicker than Tina."

They both flinched at "God" and Monique actually fell back a step. Well, she better get used to it.

"I'd invite you guys in, but I have to be—"

"Going somewhere?" Tina tilted her head. "Don't you need to feed?"

"Later, maybe."

"You haven't fed yet? And don't plan to?" Monique's eyes were big with surprise.

"I try to put it off as long as I can."

"Oh, now, surely you're not still reticent about—"

"Want to come with?" I asked abruptly, to forestall the lecture. Tina and Sinclair thought it was exquisitely stupid that I hadn't embraced my inner vampire. "I'm checking out the new house Jess picked out for us."

"You're moving?" Monique asked as I locked my house and trotted toward the car.

"Have to. Termites. And I would appreciate it if that little piece of info didn't fall into Sinclair's shell-like ears," I told Tina. "It's none of his damned business."

"Of course, Majesty."

"Quit it."

"Of course, Majesty."

"I hate you," I sighed, opening the door for Monique.

"No you don't," Tina replied, barely suppressed laughter in her tone, "Majesty."

Chapter 7

"GOODNESS!" Monique said.

"Wow," Tina said respectfully.

I slumped so hard against the steering wheel, my head activated the horn for a brief honk.

I should have known. I should have known! Summit Avenue was one of the oldest streets in St. Paul. It was absolutely packed with mansions. And 607 Summit Avenue was a doozy. White, except for black shutters. Three floors. An amazing front porch right out of *Gone with the Wind.* And the detached garage was as big as my current house.

"Dammit, dammit." I climbed out of the car, and Monique and Tina scrambled after me.

"Just how much money does Jessica have?" Tina asked in awe. It was taking forever to get to the door via the front walk.

"Too much." I was stomping so hard, I could actually feel my heels leaving marks in the concrete. I eased up. Damn sidewalk was probably five hundred years old. "Way too much."

"I think it's perfect. It suits your rank much better than—"

"Stop." I pounded on the front door, then opened it and crept in, instantly intimidated.

It was worse than I feared. The first thing I saw was the sweeping staircase, eight feet wide, shined to a high gloss, and winding up out of sight. The front hall was as big as my living room. The place smelled like wood and wax, cleaning supplies and old, old carpet.

"Jessica!" I yelled. *Ick-uh, ick-uh, ick-uh* echoed up and down the hall.

"You're going to live here?" Monique asked, goggling.

"Shit, no. Jessica!" *Ick-uh! Ick-uh! Ick-uh!*

She and Marc appeared at the top of the stairs, and galloped down to us. "Finally! You're late. What do you think?" she said. "Isn't it grand?"

"Wait'll you see the dining room table," Marc added. "It has seventeen leaves!"

"Jessica, it's too big. There's three of us, remember? How many bedrooms does this place have?"

"Eleven," she admitted. "But that way we don't have to worry about where to put up guests."

"And, we all get our own bathroom," Marc added.

"And probably your own kitchen!" Tina said, eyes gone huge as she stared at the castle Jessica had bought with the money she'd found in her car seat cushions.

Sensing my mood (not a great trick), Jessica said sternly, "Oh, come on. Open your mind. It's big, but it's just a house."

"The governor's mansion is across the street!" I yelled.

"Just look around," Marc coaxed. "You'll like it."

"You guys . . ." I heard myself getting shrill and forced my voice into the lower registers. They'd probably worked hard, and the place had cost her a bundle. The closing costs alone had probably been six figures. It made me uncomfortable as hell, but I didn't want to come off as an ungrateful jerk. "It's not a question of liking, okay? I mean, I can see it's amazing and gorgeous and stuff."

"Thank goodness," Marc said.

"It's beautiful, okay? There's nothing wrong with it. But it's a question of affordability and practicality. Come on, how much is it?"

"Well, we're renting it for now, until they track down the owner."

"Jessica . . ."

"Three thousand a week," she admitted.

I nearly fainted. "The money from my house won't even cover a year's rent!"

"So you *can* do math in your head," Marc teased. "I was wondering."

"Have you lost your mind?"

"Which one of us are you talking to?"

"Look, this is way more in keeping with your

station, anyway," Jessica said, striving to sound logical.

"What station?" I glowered at her warningly. We didn't talk about the Queen Thing. She knew I didn't like it and was trying to find a way out of it.

"You know what station," Jess said sternly. *Traitor!* "With the king dropping by—"

"Do not call him that," I said through gritted teeth.

"Wow," Marc said, peering at me. "Your eyes are getting all red again. And . . ." He looked past me. I'd heard Monique and Tina back up a step, but I was too irked to care.

"Sinclair, all right? With Sinclair and Tina and . . . and other people"—she nodded at Monique—"well, you really need a decent house. Something that shows people—"

"That my roommate pays all my living expenses. Come on, this place isn't me."

"It's private . . . we're the last house on the block, and the only thing in the back yard is the Mississippi River. It's large and private, and there's a terrific security system in the garden. And you need privacy, Bets, even if you won't admit why. And it's big enough for you to entertain."

"Can't we just get a condo in downtown Minneapolis or something?" I whined.

"Vampire queens do not live in condos." Monique said it, but Tina and Jessica nodded emphatically.

"Look, we gotta live somewhere," Marc broke in. "Right? I mean, your house is gonna collapse in on itself if those bugs keep chomping. So, give the place a try for a few weeks. That's all we're asking."

Sure they were. Like I was going to pack and move my stuff twice in the same season. Jessica was bossy, which I was used to and could fight, but Marc was the voice of reason, against which I had no defense.

"You have to admit," Tina added helpfully, "it's an amazing house."

"So? If I'm the queen, how come I don't get to make any of the rules?"

Jessica grinned. "It's not your worry. We'll keep you informed."

"It's like, Jessica's the Bruce Wayne to your Batman," Marc added. "You can go out and fight crime, and she can pay the bills."

"Bruce Wayne and Batman were the same guy, idiot."

Jessica and Tina laughed together, which was annoying. At least Monique was remaining respectfully silent.

"Hi, Tina, I didn't get a chance to say howdy before," Marc said. He put out his big paw and shook Tina's teeny delicate hand. It was almost funny. I mean, Marc was tall, slender, and in pretty good shape, and he towered over Tina. But Tina and Monique could break all the bones in his hand with a single squeeze. And he knew it. Jessica did, too. They didn't care, either.

They were adjusting to this vampire stuff a lot faster than I was.

"Give me the tour," I said, surrendering. Marc

was right. We had to live somewhere. And Jessica could buy every house on the block by barely cracking her credit line at the bank. There were lots of reasons to complain, but her financial situation wasn't one of them. "Let's see what you've signed me up for."

TINA and Monique left when the real-estate agent arrived, which was just as well. One hungry bloodsucker was plenty for the tour.

The agent was a perfectly pleasant older woman with gray hair and a truly awful tweed suit (in July!). But she scored points because, even though we all knew she was looking at a hefty commission, she didn't slobber all over us. And she knew plenty about the house. Marc whispered to me that she was probably around when it was built in 1823.

I *hee-heed* into my palm while May Townsend ("Just call me May-May, dear.") droned on about the exquisite woodwork, the fine craftsmanship, the fact that termites hadn't devoured the place, the pure privilege it was for low-life primates like us to walk on the hallowed floors. I thought about eating her, but frankly, the tweed smelled. She must have had a cedar closet at home.

"As I told you over the phone," May-May was saying while we trudged down from the third floor to the second, "most of the furniture comes with the house. The owners are in Prague and, frankly, would be interested in selling."

"We're renting," I said firmly, before Jessica could say anything.

"Very well, dear. This is the master bedroom," she added, opening the door to soaring ceilings, a bed the size of my kitchen, and huge windows. "It's been fully updated and the attached bath has a Jacuzzi, pedestal sink, and—"

"I call it!" Marc said loudly.

"Like hell," Jessica snapped. "I think the person who stands a chance of actually entertaining in their room should get it."

"Well, that lets Betsy and you out," Marc sneered. "When was the last time you got laid?"

"None of your damn business, white boy."

"Hand-stenciled wallpaper, unique to the time period, and note the gold leaf in the corners—"

"Since I've been shanghaied into this place," I interrupted, while May-May droned on about the authentic wood in the authentic floorboards, "I'll take the master bedroom. It's not like you guys don't have a dozen other ones to choose from."

"Ten," May-May corrected.

"Whatever."

"No fair!" Marc cried.

"It's that, or back to Termite Central." Finally, I was throwing my weight around . . . and actually getting my way! "Uh, hey, Marky-Marc, why don't you and May-May go check out the pedestal sink?"

"Why? If I don't get to use it, I—hey!" I gave him a gentle shove in the direction of the bathroom, sending him sprawling, and the real-estate agent dutifully followed. I didn't care if Marc heard, but my undead state was none of May-May's business.

"Uh, Jess," I asked quietly, "who's gonna take care of this mountain? Marc and I work nights, y'know, and you weren't exactly born with a silver broom in your mouth."

"I'll get a couple of housekeepers," Jessica assured me. "And we'll get someone to take care of the lawns and garden."

"I can take care of the lawn!" Marc yelled from the bathroom.

"Oh, you're gonna mow two acres every week?" Jessica yelled back. "And stop eavesdropping! I'm trying to have a private conversation here!"

"Maybe I will! Mow, I mean."

"Let's try to keep the helpers to a minimum," I said anxiously.

"Don't worry, Bets. No one's gonna find out unless you tell them."

"Find out what?" Marc asked, coming back into the room.

"That she's as dumb as she looks," Jessica said cheerfully, neatly avoiding my kick.

"Ready to inspect the first floor?" May-May asked brightly. I wasn't, but trailed behind them dutifully.

Chapter 8

JESSICA was as good as her word. I hadn't even gotten unpacked before I started seeing people in and out of the house, or Vamp Central, as Marc liked to call it. There were at least three housekeepers and two gardeners; Jessica hired them from The Foot, her nonprofit job-finding organization, so it worked out well for everybody.

The fridge was constantly full of pop, iced tea, cream, veggies, and supper fixings. The freezer bulged with ice cream and frozen margaritas. But the helpers were so circumspect, I hardly ever saw them. And if they thought it was weird that I slept all day and was out all night, nobody ever said anything to my face.

It was funny how much unpacking depressed me. We'd been in such a hurry to get out of Termiteville, I'd sort of thrown my stuff into boxes without really thinking about it. But while I was finding places to put things away, I was forced to really look at the junk I'd gathered over a lifetime.

The clothes and shoes and makeup weren't such a big deal, though I was so pale these days, I hardly ever wore anything but mascara. The books were something else.

My room had, among other things, amazing bookcases built into the corner, and while I was unpacking boxes and putting books away, I realized the gap between my old life and my new one had gotten huge without my noticing. It had been such a crazy summer, I hadn't really noticed that there hadn't been time to do any re-reading of old favorites. And now there never would be.

All my favorites: the Little House series, all of Pat Conroy's work, Emma Holly's erotica, and my cookbook collection—they were useless to me now. Worse than useless . . . they made me feel bad.

I loved *Beach Music* and *The Prince of Tides* because not only could Pat Conroy write like a son of a bitch, he had the soul of a gourmet chef. The man could make a tomato sandwich sound like an orgasm you ate. And my days of eating tomato sandwiches were long gone.

How many times had I escaped to my room with a book to avoid my stepmother? How many times had I bought a cookbook because the glorious color pictures literally made me drool? But it was done, now. Tom, Luke, Savannah, Dante, Mark, Will, and the Great Santini were all lost to me. Not to mention

The All-American Cookie Book, Barefoot Contessa Parties, and all of Susan Branch's stuff.

I put the books away, spine-side in, so I wouldn't have to look at the titles. Normally I kept too busy to feel bad about being dead, but today wasn't one of those days.

I saw the kid for the first time when I was vacuuming the inside of my closet. This was the third time in five minutes—no way was I just dumping my shoes into a two hundred year old closet that smelled like old wood and dead moths. Thank goodness I didn't have to breathe!

Handi-vac in hand, I backed out of the closet on my knees and nearly bumped into her. She was curled up like a bug in the chair beside the fireplace. One of fourteen. Fireplaces, not chairs. I had no idea how many chairs there were. Anyway, she was watching me and I was so startled I nearly dropped the vacuum.

"Yikes!" I said. "I didn't hear you come in."

"My mama says I'm quiet," she replied helpfully.

"You have no idea. It's tough work, sneaking up on me. Although," I added in a mutter, "more and more people seem to be doing it all the time." I raised my voice so the kid wouldn't get freaked out by the blond weirdo talking to herself. "So, your folks work here?"

"My mama used to."

"Used to? Then what are you—"

"I like your hair."

"Thanks." I patted my blond streaks and tried not to preen. Ah, dead, but I've still got it. "I like yours, too."

She was just about the cutest thing I'd ever seen. She had the face of a patient doe, all wary and cute, with big blue eyes and a spray of freckles across her nose. Her blond, curly hair was pulled back from her face in a blue bow that matched her eyes, and she was wearing striped overalls rolled to the knees, pink anklets . . . and saddle shoes!

I edged closer to get a better look at her footwear. "Aren't you bored to death?" I asked. "Clunking around in a big house like this? Where's your mom?"

"I like it here now," she replied, after giving my question some thought. "I like it when people are here."

"Well, you're gonna love it now. My friend Jessica hired a fu-uh, an army. Say, sunshine, where'd you get the shoes?"

"My mama bought them for me."

"Where?"

"The shoe store."

Rats. "I like them a lot," I said truthfully. "My name's Betsy."

"I'm Marie. Thanks for talking to me."

"Hey, I just live here, I'm not a rich snobby jerk like you're probably used to. Uh . . . do you know how to get to the kitchen from here?"

Marie grinned, showing a gap between her front

teeth. "Sure. I know all the shortcuts. There's a secret cave between the kitchen and the second dining room!"

"*Second* dining room? Never mind. Onward, Marie. I gotta get some tea in me before I do something somebody'll regret."

Before I could take her hand, I heard thundering footsteps, and then Jessica burst into the room, waving the telephone. "Gotta go—Marquette—Tina's in trouble," she wheezed, then collapsed until she was partially lying on my unmade bed. "Cripes! I think there's a thousand stairs in this place."

"You of all people don't get to complain about how big this place is. What are you talking about, Tina's in trouble?"

"Sinclair—on the phone—" She held it out to me.

I grabbed it. "This better not be a trick," I snarled into the receiver.

"Get here now."

I ran.

IT was a good trick, not screaming and then barfing when I saw what had been done to Tina. Luckily, I'd been audited (twice!), and was the child of ugly divorce proceedings, and had loads of practice keeping my dinner down.

"Another one of your tiresome ploys for attention," I said.

Tina tried a smile, and I hoped she'd knock it off

soon. Half her face was in tatters. In fact, half of her bad self was in tatters. She floated listlessly in the tub, which was full of pink water.

Don't ask me why, but when you immerse a sick vamp in water and add baking soda, they get better quicker. Amazing! The stuff can make cakes rise and de-stink refrigerators. It made no sense to me, but I was pretty new to the game to be questioning undead physics.

"Jeez . . ." I croaked the word out, then cleared my throat. "Who did this? Are you—of course you're not okay, but—does it hurt?"

"Yes."

"What happened?"

"Just that whole tiresome humans killing vamps thing," she replied.

That stung. "Well, shit, Tina, I didn't think they were going after the good ones!" While I was waving my arms around and generally working up a good spate of hysterics, Sinclair appeared with his usual spooky speed and grabbed my wrist.

I had time to say, "Wha—?" before he nicked my wrist with the knife I belatedly noticed he was holding. "Ow!" I said, yanking my wrist away, but it was all for show. It was so fast, and the knife was so sharp, I'd barely felt it. Well, at least he didn't bite me. "You want to ask before you start gouging me?"

Tina turned her head away and ducked under water. "And you stop that!" I said, bending over the tub and gingerly prodding her head. I wiped my wet hand off on my jeans. Yech! "I know what I'm supposed to do, dammit. It's just nice to be asked, is all," I added, glaring at Finklair.

"Stop wasting time," he said, typically stone-faced, but his eyes were kind of squinty. I knew he adored Tina. She had made him, and they had a bond I respected, even if I didn't understand it, and thought it was extremely weird. "Let her feed. Now."

"No," Tina gurgled from the bottom of the tub.

"I said I'd do it," I snapped. "Will you sit up so we can get this over with?"

A bubble appeared, but Tina didn't move.

"This is your fault," Sinclair said coldly. The situation was so alarming, I just now noticed he was wearing cherry red boxers and nothing else. "Now fix it."

"My fault? I'm not the one who decided to give Tina a haircut . . . all over! Don't get pissed at me. I came as soon as you asked me to. Not that you exactly asked."

His hand clamped onto my shoulder, which instantly went numb. "Tina is well aware of your childish aversion to blood drinking. She's playing the martyr, and I won't have it."

"Hey, I'm with you! Get her out of there and let her chomp away. I'm on your side."

If he'd been alive, his face would have been the color of an old brick. Each word was forced out through his teeth. "She will not obey me in this."

"Oh, so that's why your boxers are in a bunch? Great color, by the way, they really bring out your—

ow! Lighten up, I think I just lost all the feeling in my left arm."

"Fix it," he said implacably.

I kicked the tub. "Tina, get out of there."

A sullen glug.

"This is the queen speaking!" I managed not to laugh. Queen of shoes, maybe! "Now sit up, will you?"

"Don't ask," Sinclair hissed in my ear. "Command."

"Stop that, it tickles. Teeee-naaaa!"

She sat up. "I don't want you to," she lied. "You think it's barbaric."

"Stop being such a baby," I said, though she was one hundred percent right. "What's the alternative? You live in the tub like an undead anatomy project and slowly heal over the next six months? The maids will have a fit."

Her nostrils flared and I realized that blood had been trickling down my fingers the whole time I was arguing. I turned around, put my hands on his rock-hard chest, and pushed and kicked and shoved until I finally slammed the bathroom door in his face.

"I really can't stand that guy," I sighed, rolling up my sleeve.

"Liar," she said, and grinned at me.

"Could you not do that until your face grows back? No offense."

"Oh, Majesty," she sighed as I knelt by the tub. "I'm so sorry to ask this of you."

"Don't be a moron. I'm just glad you're alive, so to speak."

She gripped my arm and lapped the blood off my fingers, then sucked on my wrist until I couldn't see tendons or raw wounds, until she was beautiful again. It didn't take long. I was always amazed at how quickly vampires healed. It rarely took more than a few minutes. And, weirdly, my blood sped things up considerably. If Tina had fed off a human, it might have taken the better part of the night to recover. More crap I didn't understand . . . and frankly, I was afraid to ask too many questions. Tina might answer them.

"So," I said brightly. "Got any other plans for the evening?"

"After a near-death experience, I like to relax by scrubbing a tub."

"I'd help, but forget it. I've got nineteen of my own to worry about."

Chapter 9

We stepped out of the bathroom just as what's-her-face, the cutie from the other day, rushed into the suite.

"Tina, thank goodness!" she cried, her shiny blond hair in wild disarray. She looked and smelled like she'd been rolled in a McDonald's Dumpster. A mustard packet was sticking to her left cheek. "I thought they'd killed you!"

She ran to Tina and sort of fell on her, hugging her and kissing her. Yech. Good thing Tina wasn't dressed yet; she'd never get those stains out. I gathered from the babbling that the bad guys had jumped both of them, but Tina had led them away from Monique.

"Dumbass," I commented.

"I quite agree," Sinclair said, scowling. He rooted around and found one of his robes for Tina, which he held open for her. When she had it tied around her, she pretty much disappeared into fluffy black terrycloth. "You should have both stood your ground—or both run."

"I know, I know," Monique interrupted before Tina could open her mouth. "I wanted to fight but Tina—"

"And you shouldn't have left my friend and saved yourself," Sinclair continued in a voice that made dry ice seem warm and accommodating.

We all gulped. Then I patted Sinclair's arm. "All's well and all that, Eric. Everybody's okay. That's the important thing. Right? Eric?"

His eyes uncrinkled and he almost smiled as he looked down at me. "Why do you only call me by my first name in moments of crisis?"

"Because that's about the only time I don't feel like strangling you," I said truthfully. "Now don't fuss at Monique. Tina's a grown woman—a very grown woman, I might add, she's, like, a hundred years old, and if she wanted to play decoy that's her lookout."

Monique didn't say anything, but she threw me a look of pure gratitude.

"The important thing," I said emphatically, "is getting to the bottom of this. Tina's one of the good guys. She didn't deserve to have some vampire hunter after her. So I guess we better figure out why." Did I really just say we had to get to the bottom of this? I felt so stupid, bossing around people who were at least fifty years older than me.

Now if I could only remember where I'd put the memo Tina gave me . . .

"Attend, please," Sinclair said, and grabbed my elbow. Eh? He pulled me across the room and through the far door, which he promptly shut.

"What?" I whined.

"You have decided to hunt down the killers?"

"Killers, plural? Yikes. I mean, sure, I guess."

"You require my help?"

"Yes," I said, not liking where this was going. "Are we going to hang out in the dark and ask each other obvious questions? Because this is weird, bordering on creepy."

He smirked at me and held out something. I looked at it. It was one of the hotel's drinking glasses.

"What's—oh."

What had I said at Macy's? "I'd rather eat glass than take your help."

Well, shit.

"Fine," I said, grabbing the glass. God knew when he'd palmed the thing, the sneaky motherfucker. "Here goes." I stared at it. I had no idea if biting into it would hurt. But I was about to find out. At the very least, gulping down chunks of glass would make me throw up. I mean, risotto made me puke, for crying out loud.

Never mind. Quit stalling. I raised it to my mouth, closed my eyes, opened my mouth . . . and bit down on air.

Sinclair was holding the glass again. It was

uncanny how quickly he could move. He was like a magician. An evil magician in boxers. "You were really going to eat it?"

"I *said,* didn't I?"

"You're either the most amazing woman I have ever known—"

"Well." I patted my bangs back into place and smiled modestly.

"Or the most asinine."

"I hate you."

"You keep saying that," he said, drawing me close. For a wonder, I let him. Long night. Plus, he smelled great. And felt great. Cherry boxers. Yum. He dropped a kiss to the top of my ear and I effectively fought a shiver. "But you keep coming back."

"Curiosity killed the cat."

"Not yet. Come, let's rejoin the others."

"Yes," I said, massively disappointed he hadn't been more grabby, and mad at myself for being disappointed. "Let's."

"FOUR," Tina said. "Four dead so far. Again, I mean."

"I, uh, lost my memo."

She made a sound that was suspiciously like a snort. "Fine, I'll sum up for you. A group of humans has been going around targeting lone vampires and cutting off their heads, or staking them, or both."

Ick. Both?

Monique spoke up. "At least we learned something: it's not one person, it's a team."

"I never thought it was one person," Sinclair said.

"No, I wouldn't think so, either. I mean, come on. One regular guy or gal wreaking all this havoc? No chance." I stretched out my feet. Ack! Scuffed toes! I'd have to give this pair away. "How do we know it's not a group of *vamps*?"

"Blood samples found at the scene were live."

"Oh, ugh!" I cried. "You mean, if someone took my blood right now—"

"You'd be dead. At least, under a microscope. Try to stay focused, Elizabeth."

"I am. Yuck-o. Do we know why? Other than the obvious."

"The obvious?" Monique asked, looking cutely confused.

"Vampires are assholes." At their stares, I elaborated. "Look, I'm sorry, but it's true. You guys grab poor unsuspecting slobs off the street and chomp away. I'm amazed this hasn't happened earlier."

"It's happened," Sinclair said coolly, "all through the ages." He'd slipped on a pair of black slacks, but was still disturbingly shirtless. "And no one in this room behaves in such a fashion."

"You gotta admit, that makes us pretty rare."

"No, I don't think so," Monique said seriously. "Most vampires outgrow the need for the hunt. It's much easier to keep sheep."

"To what?"

I saw Tina make a slashing motion across her throat, and Sinclair shake his head; Monique was oblivious. "Sheep!" she said brightly. "You know. Two or three people who are devoted to you and let you drink whenever you need to."

"We're getting off the subject," Sinclair said quickly.

"The hell we are!"

"Later, Majesty," Tina said, glaring at Monique, who was looking amazed. "You can tell us all how awful we are *later*."

"How can we draw this team out into the open?" Tina asked.

"Well, bait, of course," Monique said.

Sinclair nodded approvingly. "They appear to strike every other Wednesday, for some reason."

"Maybe they all have jobs," I said, "and they can only get Wednesdays off."

"More likely," Sinclair said kindly, "those days are significant. For example, they might be on the occult calendar."

"So," Tina continued, "two weeks from now, we'll see if we can't catch them."

I barely contained my sneer. "Just like that, eh?"

"Well," Tina said reasonably, "chances are, they're not a bunch of old folks. The attacks are too ferocious and quick, for one thing. It's probably a bunch of young adults . . . I'll bet a thousand dollars not one of them is legal drinking age."

"Did you see any of them?" Monique asked.

"Too busy fighting, and running. They were well equipped, I'll tell you that much. I certainly did not linger."

"Good thing," I said, impressed. "I mean, even with not lingering, you got ripped up pretty good. I'm really glad you're okay."

"Why, Majesty," Tina teased, "I didn't know you cared."

"Cut that out, you slut." Tina had made no secret of the fact that she'd jump into my bed anytime. This rattled me, because A) I was straighter than a laser beam, and B) even laser beams get curious. One time in college, a bunch of my sorority sisters and I got really drunk and . . . well, anyway, sometimes I was curious. Best to keep her at arm's length. I had enough trouble keeping Sinclair out of my bed. "Your seductive ways won't work on me."

"Weapons?" Sinclair asked with a trace of impatience.

"Guns, stakes, crossbows, knives, masks. But as I said, I'm sure they're young. They felt young. They moved young, and smelled young."

"Smelled?" I asked.

"Lots of Stridex," she explained.

I stomped on the giggle that wanted out. Killer teens with acne! Sounded like a movie of the week.

"So right away, we've got an advantage."

"We do?"

"We're older, smarter, and trickier," Sinclair said, sounding way too smug for my taste.

Tina and Monique nodded.

I rolled my eyes. “Well, then, those poor guys don’t have a chance, do they?”

“Exactly,” he replied, totally missing my sarcasm.

Chapter 10

"MARIE!" I yelled. "Are you here?"

I doubted it. It was almost eleven o'clock at night. But her folks kept odd hours, because she usually—

"Hi."

"Oh, good." I popped out of my closet. "Have you seen my purple Arpels?"

"Are they the ones that look like fairy shoes, or the ones that look like ballet slippers?"

"Slippers."

"Uh-huh. The left one is under your sink, and the right one is under the bed."

"Dammit!"

"Well, you were so tired last night," Marie soothed. The kid loved overalls and hairbands; she was always dressed the same way. Must be a stubborn little tic at home. "You just sort of threw everything off you and fell into the bed."

"Stop spying on me, you little turd."

She giggled. "Don't call me that!"

"Yeah, yeah." I hunted around-lo! My shoes were exactly where she'd said. "Where is everybody?"

"Um . . . Dr. Marc is working, and Jessica's sleeping."

"Oh." Bo-ring.

"There's new stuff in the kitchen," she said helpfully. "Jessica told the pantry manager to get you some white tea, and she picked up fresh cream at the farmer's market."

"Really? D'you know how rare and expensive white tea is? I've been dying to try it. Oooh, and fresh cream! Come down, I'll fix you a cup, too."

She shook her head, which didn't surprise me. Marie was one painfully shy kid. Except around me, for some reason.

I quickly got dressed in khaki shorts, a red sleeveless mock turtleneck, and slipped into black flats. I ran a brush through my hair. It was staying exactly shoulder-length, and my highlights were staying exactly as high-lit as they'd been the day I died. One less thing to worry about. Besides, I was too chicken to try a haircut—what if I was stuck with it forever? Well, maybe a trim . . .

"I'll bring up a cup for you," I promised on my way out the door.

"I'm not thirsty," she called after me.

It took ten minutes to find the kitchen. I'd been living here for days, and still got lost. Thank God for my vampire nose, or I'd probably never have found it.

There was a note from Jessica on the table.

Bets, the owner called again. VERY anxious to sell to us. Keeps dropping the price. I'm seriously considering it. What do you think? J.

"I think it's too expensive, is what I think," I said aloud. Might as well have the argument by myself. It was the only way I'd win. "The three of us rattle around in here like dried peas in an empty can. Also, I'm getting sick of the smell of old wood."

"Bitch, bitch, bitch," Jessica yawned, slouching into the kitchen in her jade green silk pajamas. They set off her ebony skin superbly. Bitch.

"Well, it's true." I didn't add that the place was starting to grow on me, and for once, it was nice to have all the closet space I needed. "Can't sleep?"

"No, I set my alarm so I could talk to you."

"Oh. Thanks. But you need your sleep."

She shrugged. "I'll take a nap this afternoon. You're not working tonight, right?"

"Nope, I've got the next two days off. Although how Macy's will run without me remains a mystery. Are you really thinking about buying this place?"

"If the owner keeps dropping the price, it's a major steal. And you have to admit, it's beautiful."

"Agreed." I poured myself a glass of chocolate milk. Screw tea . . . took too long. "Beautiful and big. I may have to buy more shoes just to fill up my closet."

"God help us. So, what's new? Besides the fact that you're the only vampire in the world with a milk mustache?"

"Well, we've got some little scumballs killing vamps, and I was kind of torn about that until they tried to take out Tina—"

"She okay?"

"She's fine now." I omitted the gross blood drinking details. "My boss is going on vacation and is leaving me in charge of the department."

"God help us."

"Oh, quit saying that. And we're setting a trap for the killers the day after tomorrow. Also, I'm thinking of calling Child Services for Marie."

Jessica yawned and got up to make coffee. "Who?"

"This little cutie who's always hanging around. I don't mind, she's not bratty or anything, but cripes, the kid's *always* here. No matter what time it is. I'm sure her dad means well, taking her on his jobs, but this is ridiculous."

"Well, don't go flying off the handle and getting Child Services involved. You could call Detective Nick, maybe have him— No, don't glare. You're right, bad idea."

"It makes me nervous enough knowing we're living in his jurisdiction. I keep expecting him to show up on our doorstep yelling, 'You're dead and I forgot all about it!' " I shivered.

"He doesn't have a chance against Sinclair wiping his memory. But back to the kid . . . I could talk to her dad," she suggested. "Who is he?"

That stumped me. "You know, I never found out. I'll go ask her. She's probably still in my room. I'm sure the little brat's trying my shoes on when I'm not there."

I hurried back to my room, but Marie was gone, and didn't come out when I called her.

Chapter 11

"BUT why do *I* have to be bait?" I whined.

"Well, you fit the profile."

"What, I'm a vampire?"

"Yes," Monique said.

"I'm the *only* vampire who can do this?"

"Yes," Tina said.

"I don't care for this idea myself," Sinclair said. Yay, Sinclair!

"If I'm bait, that will seem awfully suspicious," Tina said. "The same with Monique. We barely got away, but now we're strolling around, unconcerned? Unlikely. And Eric, you're a little too formidable to be really good bait."

"Thank you," he said.

"Barf," I said. "Aren't there any other vampires you can pick on?"

"Well, there's Sarah . . . but she keeps pretty much to herself. She has for the last fifty years."

"Who's S—"

"And . . . you *are* the queen," Monique interrupted apologetically. "It's sort of your responsibility."

"Scratch the 'sort of'," Tina replied, "and replace it with 'entirely'."

"Whatever happened to 'they will come over you over my dead body, your Majesty?' I mean, jeez, that was only three months ago."

"That was different," Tina said with maddening calm. "You were unaware of your responsibilities then."

"Oh, blow me. Okay, okay, I'll do it. I assume I'll have back-up?"

"Of course!" Monique said warmly. I smiled at her. At last, someone who appeared to care if I was chopped into pieces. "We'll all be watching and waiting. And if the four of us can't handle a group of youths . . . well, we should all just stake ourselves right now."

"Pass," I said, although, worriedly, Tina and Sinclair were nodding. "Okay. What do I do?"

SIX hours later, I'd had enough. "This isn't working!" I yelled. "And the sun's coming up soon! A total wasted evening, losers!"

Sinclair materialized out of the shadows, effectively scaring the crap out of me. While I gasped and grabbed my chest, he said, "It appears you are correct. We'll have to try again later."

"Well, dammit," Tina said from behind me. I yipped and spun around while she continued. "I want to get these little thugs *now*."

"Soon," Sinclair soothed. He slung a companionable arm around her shoulder. He practically had to bend over to do it; she was really short. "Let's head back to the hotel and get some rest. Where's Monique?"

"Here," she said from across the street. She quickly crossed against the light—vampires were total renegades—and joined our little huddle. "This is unfortunate. I had hoped—"

"Next time," Sinclair said.

"Oh, crap! We're gonna trash another evening by doing this again?" I grumped. "Gosh, I can't wait. Remind me to get that night off, by the way."

Sinclair muttered something in response, but I didn't catch it. Lucky for him.

"Great shoes," Monique said, pointing.

"Yes," I said, pleased. I was dressed in black—a cliché, but it seemed appropriate for the evening shenanigans—except for my shoes. They were clear Lucite wedges with a butterfly in each heel. Normally I try to avoid plastic shoes, but this time I made an exception. "Aren't they great? Sixty-nine ninety five, with my discount."

"Are those real bugs?" Tina asked.

"No," I said, offended.

"Oh, that's right. You're in P.E.T.A."

"Not anymore. They were getting a little extreme. I mean, I'm as against spraying shaving cream into a rabbit's eyes as the next person. But they're trying to prevent AIDS research, which I think sucks."

"How nice," Sinclair said silkily, "that your politics are as changeable as your wardrobe."

"Uh . . . thanks?" *Was that a compliment?* "But I still wouldn't walk around with real bugs in my shoes."

"Are they comfortable?" Monique asked. "They're so high."

"Comfort is irrelevant! A small price to pay."

"This is enthralling," Sinclair said, "but the sun will be up soon, and I would rather not be burned alive while you ladies discuss footwear."

"Picky, picky. I'll see you guys later."

"I'll walk you to your car," he said quickly.

I laughed. "Why? What could possibly happen to me? The bad guys aren't coming out tonight . . . or if they did, it wasn't around here."

He hesitated for a long moment—had he been hoping for a grope in the parking garage?—then said, "Very well. Good night."

" 'Night. G'night, Tina. Bye, Monique."

Five minutes later, I was in the US Bank parking ramp. My car was the only one on level three. Good thing I was already dead, or I'd be really creeped out. Minneapolis was pretty low-crime compared to most cities, but it didn't do to tempt fate.

I unlocked my car and was about to open the

door when I noticed— Argh! Was that a *scuff* across my toes? Two pairs in one week! My vampire lifestyle was ruining my footwear, and I just would not stand for it.

I bent over to get a closer look, and heard a *whummm-thud!* I straightened up in a hurry and saw a thick wooden arrow quivering in the metal between my window and the roof of the car.

I whirled. There was a kid—eighteen, nineteen—standing beside one of the concrete pillars, holding a crossbow. I heard the click as he popped another arrow into place, and sidestepped just as the punk blew out my driver side window.

"Cut that out!" I shouted. "What's the matter with you?"

Move.

I ducked again, and the kid jumped behind the pillar as two more arrows sailed past him. Great. There was one behind me, too.

"What, you were too good for our trap?" I called out. "I wasted my entire evening and you show up *now?* Next time"—I could actually see the kid's arrow coming at me in not-quite-slow motion, and sidestepped again. Guess my undead adrenaline was kicking in—"make an appointment."

"Give it up, you vampire whore," someone called from behind me.

"Oh, that's nice," I snapped. "You don't even know me!"

I heard muffled footsteps. They were good, I hadn't even noticed I was walking into an ambush.

But now I was noticing everything. I figured there were at least three people on this level with me, maybe four.

I had the strong urge to move again—thank you, inner voice—and this time three bullets stitched my car door. Then another smacked into my shoulder.

"Owwwww!" I complained. It felt like getting bopped with a baseball bat. It hurt for a few seconds, then my shoulder went numb. "Lucky for you guys I've got a million other T-shirts at home. What did I ever do to you?"

The ones behind me were muttering to themselves, and the kid by the pillar—a blue-eyed blonde right out of Surfing Central Casting—looked amazed. He stared and stared, appearing to be waiting for something. What? For me to blow up? Were the bullets special?

"Duds," the woman called from somewhere.

Finally, he said, "Stand still, you fucking bloodsucker."

"Are you on drugs? Do I have Giant Moron written on my forehead?"

"No," my would-be killer admitted.

"And will you stop with the wrecking of my car? I have to make this one last at least another year." Luckily, Fords were built tough. "Who are you jerk offs, anyway?"

"We're the Blade Warriors," a woman called from behind me. She was pretty well hidden; I had no idea what she was wearing. I rolled my eyes, and the kid by the pillar stopped in mid-reload to stare at me again. "We kill vampires."

I snorted. Teenagers! Well, at least they'd stopped shooting at me. "The Blade Warriors? Seriously? You guys actually thought that up and said, 'yeah, that name doesn't blow, we'll go with that one'?"

There was an embarrassed silence.

"And as far as killing vampires goes," I continued smugly, "you're sort of sucking at it. How much ammo have you wasted on me?"

"You'd know about sucking," Blondie sneered.

"Hey, I'm not the one running around in Kevlar with crossbows in the middle of the night like a geek loser. And four against one? Not *too* lame."

"But you're a vampire!" the woman protested. She was about ten feet closer. Oh-ho. Keep the dead chick talking while the other three sneak up on me. "You kill people!"

"No I don't. I've only killed one person in my whole life, and he was already dead. I *told* you guys you didn't know anything about me. What, because I'm a vampire I automatically deserve to be shot with arrows?"

"Well . . . yes."

"Bullshit. You're teenagers, but I'm not trying to kill *you*. Although if you keep shooting up my car," I muttered, "I might."

Having finished my speech, I figured it was time to get gone before my luck ran out. Thank goodness,

I was parked on the right side of the ramp. I swiftly crossed the six feet to the wall, dodging another bullet and two arrows on the way, and without another word to the Loser Warriors, vaulted over the ledge and plummeted three stories to the street below.

Chapter 12

I limped down the street, grabbed the first homeless guy I saw, apologized profusely, and hauled him behind a dumpster for a rejuvenating snack. As always, drinking blood felt physically wonderful, while emotionally I was disgusted with myself.

After a few seconds (it never took long), I left my smiling, sleeping blood donor asleep on a pile of cardboard. It was a warm night; he'd be okay. Unless you knew he was there, you couldn't see him.

My shoulder healed like magic before I even left the alley, and I was amazed to feel the bullet pop free of my flesh and fall into my bra.

I fished it out and stared at it, but I don't know a bullet from a dildo, so I tucked it back in and resolved to show it to Sinclair later. Or maybe Nick Barry . . . a cop would know all sorts of stuff about bullets. If I dared involve him in this.

I made it home just before dawn—thank goodness for late night taxis!—and realized when I tried to pay the fare that I'd left my purse in my car. So I zapped him with the old vamp mojo, ignoring the stab of guilt, and he drove off thrilled to his toes.

There was, of course, the expected uproar when I walked in. Marc and Jessica were both yelling at me at once, and while Jessica punched buttons on her cell phone, Marc nagged me into stripping off my T-shirt so he could check my wound.

"Huh," he said, poking my shoulder like I was a side of beef. "I don't see a thing."

I coughed but didn't elaborate on how I'd cured myself. "Who are you calling?" I asked Jessica.

"You know who," she said, then barked into the phone, "Betsy was attacked. She's here now."

"Aww, no, not Sinclair! That's all I need." I looked at my watch. "He probably won't have enough time to get here, anyway."

"Yeah, he's pretty helpless, that one," Marc said. He wadded up my shirt. "Might as well toss this, chickie, it's ruined. What was it like, getting shot?"

"What kind of a dumbass question is that from a guy who went to medical school? It hurt!"

"I mean, is it different for a vampire, do you think? I've seen lots of bullet wounds at the hospital, but none that healed in an hour."

"How should I know? I've never been shot before. I mean, I could see the bullets coming at me—"

"Cool, like in *The Matrix*?"

"No. They were like baseballs thrown hard. I could dodge them, but I really had to be on my toes."

"Thank God you're all right," Jessica said. I blushed with pleasure, and then she wrecked it by adding, "you idiot. What were you *thinking?*"

"Hey, don't yell at me! I was *thinking* of going to my car and driving home," I said. "I'm the victim. So what, exactly, is my crime?"

"I'm gonna strangle that Sinclair," she muttered. When Jess got mad she sort of did this thing where she sucked on her cheeks, which threw her cheekbones into sharp relief. She looked like a pissed-off Egyptian queen who needed a few milkshakes. "Dragging you into this . . . putting you in danger . . ."

"This wasn't part of me being bait. This was after. The . . ." I could barely get it out without giggling. "The Blade Warriors were waiting for me in the parking ramp."

Marc's eyebrows shot up and he and Jessica traded a glance.

"I know how it sounds," I said.

"Bad," Jessica replied.

"*Real* bad," Marc elaborated.

"I was talking about their name, but you're right, that's not too cool. An ambush. Huh. Look, I'm going to grab a quick shower; I feel sort of yucky. We'll talk more in a few minutes, okay?"

Annoyingly, they waited outside my bathroom while I freshened up. At least Marie wasn't here—it would have been too awful to explain the evening's occurrences to a little kid.

I stepped out of the bathroom in clean cotton shorts and a new T-shirt, and started back downstairs. Jessica and Marc didn't wait, they pelted me with questions during the long journey to the main living room.

"How did you get away? Tell me everything," Jessica ordered finally, when she noticed I was ignoring everything she and Marc were saying. "Start with, 'I went diddy-bopping out the door six hours ago like a big blond idiot,' and finish with 'and then I walked in all bloody and tired-looking'."

"Can't it wait?" I griped. "I'm just going to have to tell it all to Sinclair again. Ugh, what a night. I'll be glad when it's tomorrow. Tonight, I mean."

Just then, the front door was thrown open, hard enough to make us all jump, and lo, there was the prince of darkness.

"Are you all right?" Sinclair demanded, crossing the room in swift strides and peering at my face.

"Please, come in," I said sarcastically. "Don't forget to wipe your feet. And I'm fine. There was no need to rush over here. Where are your shoes?"

Jessica coughed. "I sort of promised him I'd keep him apprised."

I forgot about the fact that Sinclair was in a suit, a topcoat, and bare feet. "You did *what?*"

"Never mind that now," Sinclair said impatiently. He was running his hands over my face, my neck, my shoulders, my arms.

I slapped his hands away when he started to raise my shirt to look at my stomach. "No, let's talk about that *right* now." Before I could work up a good rant, I realized I was suddenly very tired. Extremely tired. I shook my head to try to throw it off, and realized that it was a lot lighter outside. "Uh-oh," I managed, just as Sinclair and the living room tipped away from me, and the carpet rushed up to my face.

"I hate that," I said, exactly fifteen hours later. I opened my eyes and was startled to see Sinclair with his jacket off, sitting in the chair beside my bed, reading. "Jesus!"

He winced. "Please don't call me that. Good evening."

"This is so bogus! How come *you* don't have to sleep all day?"

"I'm quite a bit older than you are. Now." He slapped the book shut. I saw it was one of Jessica's collection of antique school books. Dumbest hobby ever, except maybe for golf. "Tell me everything that happened last night."

I ignored the command. "Did you sleep at all?" I asked suspiciously. Oh, I knew him of old.

He smirked. "I did rest beside you for a few hours."

"Pervert!"

"No, but if I was such a thing, taking advantage of you would have been simplicity itself."

"Have I mentioned how much I strongly, *strongly* dislike you?"

"Ah!" he said, looking pleased. "We're making progress. From hate to dislike."

"Strong, strong dislike. Where are my roomies? I don't want to have to tell this story a thousand times."

"We're here," they chorused, walking into my bedroom.

"And so am I," Tina added, trailing them. "Are you all right, Majesty?"

I'd given up on trying to get her to call me by my first name. I ignored Marc's chortle and replied, "I'm fine. I only got shot once."

A muscle jumped in Sinclair's cheek. Weird. I'd never seen that before. "They shot you?" he asked with scary calm.

"My car's a lot worse off than I am, believe me. Which reminds me, we have to go get it tonight. And my purse. In all the excitement—"

"From the beginning, please."

I told them. I didn't leave anything out. And nobody interrupted, not once, which was a brand new experience.

"They knew you were a vampire," Tina said when I finished. She looked very, very troubled.

"Uh, yeah. Good point. *How* did they know? I mean, most vampires don't even believe it."

"And how did they know about the other vampires?" Marc asked.

"Well, it must be . . . I mean, maybe a vampire is siccing these guys on us?" I guessed.

"Probably a vampire," Jessica said at once. "Who else would know who's dead and who's not?"

Sinclair nodded. "And they were waiting for you." He looked cool as a cucumber, but his hands kept opening and closing into fists. "They knew you were coming."

"Apparently so." I hadn't really had time to think about how weird that was. "Quit doing that, it makes me nervous. Oh! I almost forgot!"

I jumped out of bed and practically ran over to my dresser, where I'd placed the bullet after tossing my clothes in the hamper. "I have a clue!" I said proudly, holding it up.

"That's great, Nancy Drew," Marc said with fake enthusiasm.

"Shut up. Check this out, you guys." I gave it to Sinclair, who examined it briefly and passed it to Tina.

"This is a hollow-point," she said, very surprised.

"Yikes," Jessica said. "A vampire gun expert."

"I like to keep busy," she replied mildly. "I'll take a look at it later."

"I was thinking we could show it to Nick," I said.

"Detective Nick Berry? I don't think that's wise at all," Sinclair said. "Best he stays out of our business."

"He might already be in it. He pulled me over the other day and had all sorts of questions. Don't worry," I said, because Tina and Sinclair both looked alarmed, "your mojo's holding. He didn't remember about me being dead and all."

"Still, he sought you out," Tina said, looking troubled.

"It was just a coincidence," I said uneasily. "He recognized my car and pulled me over."

There was a short silence, broken by, "You should rest," Sinclair ordered, getting up from his chair. "Spend the night in bed."

"I spent the *day* in bed, and that's plenty."

He ignored me, as usual. "Tina and I will put our heads together and—"

"I'm *fine,* how many times do I have to tell you? Stop clucking. And I have to work tonight, I can't stay in bed."

"You will not be going to work."

"The hell!" I glared up at him. "Stop trying to boss me around, when are you going to learn?"

Jessica cleared her throat. "Uh, Betsy."

I ignored her. "I never listen—"

"I have learned that."

"—and it just pisses me off."

"Bets."

"Frankly, you could do worse than listening to me," Sinclair snapped back. "This *faux* independence of yours is growing tiresome."

"Faux?" I cried. That meant fake, right? Probably. Stupid French! "Listen, jerkoff—"

"Betsy!" Jessica seized my arm in a grip that would have hurt like hell if I'd been alive. "Girl talk," she said to the room at large, then dragged me into the bathroom.

I extricated myself, with difficulty, from her grasp. "What? I'm in the middle of something, here. What did you have to say to me right this second?"

She lowered her voice; we were both well aware of vampire hearing. "I wanted to stop you before you said something worse."

"Girlfriend, I haven't even gotten started—"

"Okay, I know you don't like him—or you think you don't like him, I haven't figured out which—but Bets! It was the most romantic thing ever. He caught you before you did a nosedive into the carpet. I mean, you started to go down and he *moved*. Then he sort of scooped you up and carried you up to bed, although how he knew which room was yours is sort of a mystery, and he never left your side."

"Ew."

"No, the opposite of ew. I came up to check on you guys about lunchtime and you were both . . . uh . . . dead to the world, and he had his arm around your shoulders and you were sort of cuddled into his side."

"I was not!" I said, shocked. Was I so shameless in my undead sleep?

"Bets, you totally were. And then, when I checked on you a few hours later—"

"Jeez, couldn't stay away, could you? Not too creepy."

"Hey, it's interesting. Anyway, Eric was awake, and he asked if he could borrow one of my old books, and nice as you pleased, asked for a cup of coffee."

"You're not a waitress."

"No, but I'm a good hostess. Anyway, it was . . . it was kind of nice. He was really nice. And he's nice to you."

"No, he isn't!"

"I think you should treat him better," she said firmly.

Traitor! I took a deep breath, which made me dizzy. "And *I* think . . ."

But we were interrupted by a knock on the bathroom door, so we went back out to my room. To my surprise, Sinclair and Tina were gone.

"He sort of stomped out," Marc replied in answer to my unspoken question. "And she said goodbye, very politely, and followed him." He shook his head. "Are you really going to work tonight?"

"You bet."

"It's just . . ." Marc looked worried, which for him was pretty rare. "Those warrior guys knew who you were. They might be tracking you."

That was a startling—and unpleasant!—thought. "I don't think so," I said after a minute's thought. "How would they know where I work?"

"They knew where you parked," he pointed out.

"I *have* to go. Otherwise, Finklair will think I dodged work because *he* said to."

"Perish the thought," Jessica said. "God forbid you should take the advice of an older, experienced, extremely intelligent man."

"I'd do anything that guy asked me," Marc said admiringly. "What a hunk! Oooh, and he's all intense and stern, but you just know that once you got him between the sheets—"

"Stop!" Jessica and I said simultaneously.

"You know it's true." He wiggled his eyebrows at me. "In fact, Betsy, didn't you find out for yourself not too long ago?"

"I don't want to talk about that," I said firmly. "He tricked me. He knew if we had sex, he'd be the king."

No, I didn't like to talk about it. But I sure thought about it a lot. Not only was it the most pleasurable sexual experience of my life, it had been *so* intense. Because, for a while there, while he was inside me, I was inside *him*. I could read his mind. And his thoughts . . . his thoughts had been very nice. While we were having sex, at least, he had really liked me.

Maybe loved me.

"Come on," Marc was saying in his coaxing doctor voice, "it was three months ago. And there have been compensations, right? I mean, Sinclair and Tina are cool, and it's obvious they really like you. What's so bad about that? When are you going to let it go?"

"A thousand years," I said, trying not to show how upset I was getting. Marc, who had a huge crush on Sinclair, just didn't get it. And Jessica thought I should be nice to him. Nice! "That's how long I'm stuck in this gig. Thanks to *him*."

"Well, I know, and I'm sorry. Don't cry about it," he said, kindly enough. "But there's worse things than nice vampires thinking you're in charge, right?"

"I don't want to talk about it anymore."

"Okay," Jessica said at once. She was glaring at Marc. "You don't have to if you don't want to. Look, why don't you get dressed for work? I'll make you some tea, and then we'll go get your car."

I sniffed. "Okay. Actually, I'll come down with you. I want tea right now . . . I'm dying of thirst. Don't look at me like that."

"Sorry," they said in uneasy unison.

"Oh, please. Like I'd ever bite either of you two dorks," I muttered. "I'm gonna change my clothes, and I'll be right down."

They left, and I thought I heard the front door open, but I was too annoyed to really care. More visitors—great! Well, bring it on.

I turned around to go to my dresser and nearly fell over Marie. "Jeez, don't *do* that!" I practically yelled. Okay, I did yell. "Sugar, would you mind clearing out? I've had a rotten evening and it's barely started. Go find your dad, or something."

"Sure," she said, staring at me with big, solemn eyes. "But I don't think you should open the door."

Yeah, yeah, whatever. She was gone when I came out of the bathroom, and I changed into a clean blouse, khaki shorts, and slipped on a pair of black sandals. I ran a brush through my hair and decided that would do, and decided to head downstairs.

I opened my bedroom door, and got the surprise of my life.

Chapter 13

FROM the private papers of Father Markus, Parish Priest, St. Pious Church, 129 E. 7th Street, Minneapolis, Minnesota.

Killing the Evil Ones is not as satisfying as I had assumed it would be. And I can hardly believe I am thinking such a thing, much less writing it down. When I am long dead, these papers will belong to the Holy Church. What will they think of me, and however will I explain myself to my Heavenly Father?

At first, I thought God was acting through our employer. I am beginning to wonder if that was the devil, speaking to me in the voice of my pride. Because many things I have long believed may not be true. And if that is the case, what will become of me? What will become of the children? They say all things work toward God's will . . . perhaps even the Undead do, as well.

The money, the equipment, the skills of the Blade Warriors . . . every vampire the children found was dispatched. I assumed we were doing great good. We are commanded not to kill, but are these things not already dead? I thought God was acting through me, through the children, but now . . .

It started to go bad when the two females escaped. Both were beautiful, looked young, and had the strength of ten tigers. Although we inflicted great damage on the smaller, dark one, she eluded us in the end. It was the first time we had been unable to do our duty, and it weighed heavily on the boys. Ani was more sanguine, but even she couldn't hide her distress.

Then there was the vampire in the parking garage.

Except was she?

Our employer had never been wrong. But this woman—she did not hiss and snarl when cornered, she did not try to bite. She seemed puzzled, and annoyed, and although she moved with the grace of a jungle cat she did not try any tricks of the dead—the hypnosis, the mind-bending, the seduction. Instead, she yelled at Jon and mocked the rest of us. She made us feel foolish and worse, we feared we *were* foolish. And after taunting us, instead of engaging, she fled. And we learned something more—heights are a vampire's friend.

Ani found the purse in the woman's—the *vampire's*—car. And that was another thing. This vampire had a car, a job, and a life. She was carrying full identification, right down to her library card.

Vampires, going to the library.

The name was right—Elizabeth Taylor—but nothing else fit with what we knew of the Undead.

We could all feel doubts start to creep in. In our business, that is fatal.

Jon proposed a simple yet daring plan. And so it was that the next evening, we found ourselves on Summit Avenue, in the state's capitol.

To our great surprise, the front door was unlocked. There were several cars in the driveway, and when we stepped inside we could see a cook hurrying through the entryway with bags of groceries. She gave us a single, disinterested glance and disappeared through an archway. We heard a car start outside and Wild Bill went to check. When he returned, he informed us the gardener had just left.

"Weird" was Ani's comment. She was a philosophy major at the University, and we had deep respect for her mind. "The vampire's driving a beat-up Ford, but she lives here? And what are all these people doing here? Do they know? And if they do, are they with her? Or prisoners? There aren't any marks on them, and they don't look like they've been snacked on . . ."

Before we could answer—and troubling questions they were—a lovely young African American woman came hurrying down the steps, and behind her was, of all things, a physician! He was a sharp-looking young man with dark hair, wearing light green scrubs and looking quite surprised to see us.

"Oh, great," the woman said. She was thin to the point of emaciation, but lovely just the same. Her ebony skin had reddish undertones, and her cheekbones made her look almost regal. Her eyes flashed dark fire as she hurried toward us. And, oddest of all, she seemed familiar to me. "Don't tell me, let me guess. The Blade Warriors. I have a huge bone to pick with you."

"That was our friend you ganged up on," the doctor added. He was right on her heels as they rapidly approached.

This was a bit nerve-wracking. We were quite helpless around humans—we certainly wouldn't kill *them!* But we had never met a vampire with human friends before.

And where had I seen the woman?

"Maybe they're pets," Ani muttered behind me.

"Maybe you're trespassing," the woman replied coldly. "You assholes are on private property. *Mine.* So get the hell out, unless you're here to apologize to my friend. In which case, you can still get the hell out, because we don't want to hear it."

"The door was unlocked," Jon pointed out.

"So it's not breaking and entering," the doctor said, grinning. "It's just entering."

His little joke caused most of us to relax a bit, but

the young woman remained unmoved. "You guys get out of here," she said with clear warning in her voice. "I'm going to count to three. Then I'm loading the shotgun. Then I'm filling the waterguns with bleach. Then I'm releasing the hounds. Then—"

"Jessica Watkins?" I asked, utterly surprised.

She blinked at me, just as surprised. "Yeah. So?"

"I'm Father Markus. You donated half a million dollars to my church." At last, at last I had placed her! I hadn't recognized her in faded jeans and a Gap T-shirt, because I usually saw the lady at fundraisers, when she was dressed in formal attire. "This is a surprise. It's good to see you."

Taken aback, she let me shake her hand. "Uh, yeah. Good-good to see you, too. Um. What are you doing with these idiots?"

"These are my children," I corrected her firmly.

She leered. "Oh, you're one of *those* priests, eh?"

Although the Church's reputation had suffered grievously the last few years, I did not rise to the bait. "I take care of them," I explained patiently, "and they look after me in my old age. We do God's work."

"Not today, Father! Betsy never did a single thing to any one of you. Leave her alone!"

"We're here to solve a mystery," I said. "We're not quite sure your . . . your friend is . . . is who we think she is."

"So you come to my house at night, bristling with weapons? I'm surprised you didn't show up at noon like true cowards," she said, her imperious voice dripping with scorn. She was her father's daughter, all right. The man had been known to make other CEOs cry just before taking over their companies.

"We would never," I said, offended. "Even the undead deserve to be dealt with honorably."

"Outnumbered five to one and cornered and staked to death? Father Markus, I never dreamed you were such an asshole."

How that stung! I was a good man, a good priest. I helped hunt the Undead. I saved lives. I was *not* an asshole.

As was her wont, Ani stepped in when she felt someone was being disrespectful. "Don't talk to Father Markus like that," she said in warning. She was a tall woman—easily my height—with jet-black hair cut just below her ears, and lovely, tip-tilted almond-shaped eyes. Her mother had been Japanese; she had never known her father, but from her build and coloring, we guessed he was Northern European. Her limbs were long and slender, and she was one of the fastest runners I had ever seen. She had been considering the Olympics when we found her. "Not unless you want to eat teeth."

"Ani," I murmured.

"Going to stake regular people next, you bimbo?" Jessica snapped. "You come into my house hunting my friend, you don't even knock, you bring guns and knives into my home, and now you're threatening me? Girlfriend, you should have kept your ass in bed today."

The children were shifting uneasily, and I couldn't blame them. Hunting the Undead was one thing. Arousing the ire of the city's—the state's!—wealthiest citizen was quite another. Even without her money, Jessica Watkins would have been formidable. As I said, she was her father's daughter.

"Look, let's make a deal," the doctor said, neatly breaching the awkward silence. "Father, why don't you go upstairs to Betsy's room—"

"Betsy?" I repeated.

"—and toss some of your holy water on her. That should do the trick, right?"

"Marc," Jessica began, but he shook his head at her.

"Well." I coughed. "It will likely burn her severely. It could even kill her. Or blind her. Your friend."

"It's a risk we're willing to take," the doctor said cheerfully.

"We're going with him," Jon said.

"Fine, but the toys stay down here. Just holy water. Ought to be enough for big-shit vampire killers like you guys, right?"

His words were rude, but he was still grinning at us in a friendly way. I tried to find the trap, but I couldn't see it. "Right."

"So, then. Go on up. We'll wait." He looked disturbingly cheerful, but, as I said, I couldn't see the problem.

The children dutifully unholstered guns and unsheathed knives. There was quite a pile on the lovely cherry table when they finished unloading. As for myself, my cross and holy water had always been all I needed. The Undead always went after one of the children; they tended to steer clear of me.

"Right, then." I took a deep breath. "Let's go. But first . . ." The children dropped their heads obediently, and I closed my eyes. "O Heavenly Father, please guide my hand and keep our family safe. In Your name, Amen."

"Amen," they echoed. Interestingly, the doctor and Jessica also said Amen.

"Third floor," he said helpfully. "Fifth door on the left. Watch the seventh step, it squeaks."

I couldn't help but stare at him, and knew my bewilderment must have shown on my face. Odder and odder. But we had our duty, and even had permission to finish it.

I pulled the cork from the bottle of holy water and led the way upstairs.

Chapter 14

I opened the door and, to my total amazement, got a vial full of water thrown in my face. For a moment I just sputtered. Then I started to sneeze.

Oh, great. Holy water! The stuff was worse than hot pepper. I sneezed and coughed and gasped until my vision finally cleared.

There were several people crowded in the hallway, but I focused on the tall, old one in black, the one staring at me and holding a cross out.

"Thanks very much!" I snapped. "What'd I ever do to you, jerk? Here I am, minding my own business, and you throw holy water in my face! Look at my hair! And my *shirt!* Dammit, I just put this on!" I shook water off my feet—lucky for these guys they were last season's sandals—and shouldered my way past him and the other weirdos. "Is this what they teach you in Jerkoff School? Do *I* come to *your* house and throw water on *you?*"

"We . . . uh . . ."

"Well, come on." I stomped down two levels and heard them sort of shuffling after me. Nobody was talking. Which was probably just as well, since I wasn't done yelling. "And another thing! Haven't you heard of knocking? I mean, how long were you lurking in my hallway, anyway? Not *too* creepy."

Marc and Jessica were waiting for me at the foot of the stairs. Marc was smirking, and Jessica was glaring. At least all was right with those two.

"Problems?"

"You wouldn't believe it!" I ranted. "I open the door, and big idiot in black here throws holy water on me!"

"Not surprising. Marc told him to," Jessica said.

"You *what?*"

"We weren't sure," big idiot in black said, looking confused and scared and apologetic, all at the same time. "We weren't sure . . . we thought you were a vampire."

I was a heartless denizen of the undead, and I was unmoved. Who cared if he strongly resembled somebody's grandpa? Okay, *my* grandpa. "I *am* a vampire, dumbass! I ought to pull all your teeth out and play craps with them."

"But . . . but that's impossible!" one of the dorky teens blurted. I glared at him . . . and recognized him.

They all took a big step back as I rounded on

them. "I know you guys! You're the Broody Warthogs!"

"Blade Warriors," one of them, the surfer dude from last night, corrected in a mutter.

"You shoot up my car and now you're *here?*" I whirled on Marc and Jessica. "They didn't hurt you guys, did they?"

"Never," the big idiot in black said, sounding—the nerve!—offended. "We only kill the dead."

I finally realized the black suit was actually a priest's outfit, and so resisted the urge to pull his head off his shoulders and use it as a soccer ball. Would I go to hell for calling a priest a dumbass? Even if he was one? A problem to worry about later.

"You guys . . ." I took a breath, ignoring the wave of dizziness that caused, and forced calm. "We've been looking for you guys."

"I'll bet," the woman said. She was super pretty, and big—my height—but looked mean, like a tall, evil Lucy Liu with a bad haircut. "I'll just bet."

"Hey, you think we're not gonna notice if you guys are running around slaughtering vampires?" I lied, because, of course, I hadn't. "Hardly! You're in big trouble."

Oooh, wait till Sinclair found out I caught the Word Barriers! All by myself!

"I don't think—" the priest began, trying yet again, but I was still too annoyed to let him finish a sentence.

"What's the matter with all of you? What'd I ever do to any of you?"

"Well," big idiot in black said. "Ah. That is to say . . . nothing."

"She isn't a vampire," surfer guy insisted.

"She is," shorter geek with black hair moussed in spikes and tipped in white insisted.

"Is not!"

"Is!"

"Isn't!"

"Is!"

The Lucy Liu knockoff stepped to the big table in the entryway, pulled a knife as long as my forearm out of a heroic pile of weapons, and handed it to Marc, handle first, much to his surprise. "Would you please," she asked pleasantly, "drive this into my ear until I can't hear anymore?"

I couldn't help it. I laughed. And, as always, it was hard to hold onto my mad when I was giggling. Ridiculous, but there you go.

"I still say she's not a vampire," Wild Bill, the kid who had the armadillo haircut, insisted half an hour later. He had cream on his lip, but I wasn't going to tell him.

"You'll just have to take my word for it," I said. We were in the Tea Room—one of the tea rooms—and Jessica was playing hostess to the people who had tried to kill me. Well, I guess it was slightly more civilized than biting them or pulling their arms off. "I really am. And we'd better figure out how to get along."

"You can't blame us for being surprised," Ani said. Her name was Ani Goodman. Wasn't that a great name for a vampire hunter? Give the girl a decent haircut, and she would be a force to be reckoned with. "It's just that you're awfully . . . uh . . ."

"Vain," Marc said.

"Shrill," Father Markus added.

"Annoying," Jessica piled on.

"Did someone already say vain?" Jon, the leader who looked like a surfer, said.

"You guys are hilarious." I crossed my arms over my chest and crossed my legs for good measure. "If everybody's done having a good chuckle at my expense—"

"*I'm* not done," Marc said.

"This is awkward," Father Markus said.

"No kidding!"

"Because until now, we have felt we were doing God's work."

"Oh. I thought we were still talking about me."

"I'm sure we will be, soon enough," Ani soothed, and Jessica cracked up. They traded a look, and the mood of the room shifted a bit more toward the "can't we all get along?" side.

"The vampires we killed—they were abominations." Boy, that Father Markus would *not* be shaken off a subject. "But now, given recent events . . ."

I squirmed. I knew how bad vamps could be. But I was the queen—laughable as the idea was—and I had a responsibility here. Too bad I hadn't the faintest clue what it was.

"So you guys just woke up one day and decided to start staking vampires?" Marc asked. He leaned over and stuffed half an éclair into his mouth. I nearly drooled . . . the pastries looked sooooo good. Custard squirted out the end and puddled on his plate. I looked up and realized Jon was watching me watch the pastry. I tore my gaze away and contented myself with another gulp of tea. "What, it was in your horoscope or something?"

"No," Jon said. "Father Markus knows tons of people from his parish work, people the rest of us have never met, people from all over the world."

"Well, that's true," Markus coughed modestly.

"And a few months ago he started getting these e-mails, and then money started showing up in our account for weapons and stuff, and then we'd get a list of names and addresses. Hangouts, like . . . and we'd go to work."

"How'd they know about you guys? How'd you even learn to fight?"

"They are orphans who avoided the system," Father Markus said quietly.

"So?" I asked, puzzled.

"Grew up on the streets," Ani said with her mouth full. She swallowed her sugar cookie and continued. "Good place to learn how to fight."

"I caught Jon and Bill trying to boost my tires behind the church," Markus said fondly, "and brought them under my wing. And they brought me the others."

"Awww, that's so cute. Not that we give a shit." I snickered. So much for being a good hostess. "Who's financing you?" Jessica asked.

The Weird Warriors looked at each other. "Well, the thing is," Father Markus said delicately, "we don't know. Our—"

"Puppet master," Jessica said.

"—patron wishes to remain anonymous."

Jessica rolled her eyes at Marc, who shrugged. I thought it was kind of weird, myself, but didn't say anything. With Jessica in the room, I didn't have to. "Uh-huh. So, you guys get everything you need to kill vampires, somebody just hands you all that stuff on a plate, and you don't question it, you just start killing them off?"

"We questioned it at first," Ani said. "But we were more easily persuaded when the first vampire nearly killed Drake."

"Who's Drake?"

"Drake doesn't run with us anymore. He's trying to learn how to walk again."

"Oh," Marc and I said.

"Anyway," she said briskly, "after that, it was easy. We certainly didn't question the morality of it. Most of the time when we cornered a vampire they were about to eat somebody. Or were actively hurting someone just for fun."

I squirmed, but didn't say anything.

"Until we ran into you, that is."

At last, I could say something in defense of

vampires. "Actually, until you ran into Tina and Monique. They got away, too. And FYI, they're good guys! Not that you bothered to check."

"Look, we're sorry," Jon said, crumbling his vanilla biscuit in his agitation—what was he thinking? *I* wasn't going to vacuum, that was for sure! "But who checks the bona fides of the undead? They're vampires, *ergo* they're evil, *ergo* they should be killed."

"I've got your *ergos* right here," I muttered. Unfortunately, he had a point. Not that I could tell them that. In fact, what could I tell them? Should I even be talking to them? Was I supposed to be killing them right now? I'd never killed anybody alive before.

And how could I kill them when they were drinking orange pekoe tea and eating cookies with us? Should I wait until they finished, or jump them when they were getting refills? Being a soulless denizen of the undead was *really* hard sometimes.

While I was pouring more tea and contemplating mass murder, I heard a door slam open one floor down, but didn't say anything. We had enough problems without more uninvited guests.

There was a *tap-tap* on the window behind me, and I turned. And nearly spilled my tea. Tina was looking through the window, which was disturbing because we were two stories up.

We're coming, she mouthed. *Stay calm.*

"For heaven's sake," I said, standing, crossing the

room, and opening the window. Everyone else jumped, and Jessica let out a little scream when she saw what was on the window. I realized I was the only one who'd heard Tina knock. "Come in here and have some tea like a civilized person. Eww, you're just sort of hanging on the house like a blond moth! Get in here."

She glared at me but clambered in. Then she glared at the Warriors. "We're here," she said with great dignity, "to rescue you from certain death."

"Biscuit?" Ani asked sweetly.

The door to the tea room slammed open and, big surprise, there was Sinclair. Uninvited, as usual. He didn't stand still very long; the next thing I knew he had picked Jon up and was shaking him like a broken pepper grinder.

Pandemonium. Spilled tea. Biscuits on the floor, where they promptly got stepped on and ground into the two-hundred-year-old carpet.

I jumped in front of Sinclair, arms spread, just in time to get another face full of holy water. I shook my head to clear my eyes, then grabbed Jon and wrenched him out of Sinclair's grip. A little too hard; the guy went sailing over the back of two chairs and hit the corner with a thud that shook the teacups.

"Stop it, *stop it!*" I yelled. "This isn't helping, you retard!" Then I spun and sneezed on Sinclair's lapels.

The two little guys—Wild Bill and Devo—were cowering behind Father Markus, who had his cross out, but Ani looked ready to rumble as she studied Sinclair and clutched a butter knife.

"It appears her Majesty does not need saving," Tina said, and *she* was studying Ani.

"No shit. Thanks for noticing. Why don't you guys sit down, take a load off? Have some tea, and a cookie if they aren't all squashed."

"Why," Sinclair demanded, whipping out a black handkerchief and wiping my face, "are you having tea with the vampire killers?"

"Because they're too young to drink alcohol?" I guessed.

Tina brought her hand up to cover a grin.

"Hey, I recognize you!" Ani said suddenly, staring at Tina.

"No you don't," I said quickly. "Never seen her before. Got her mixed up with another bloodsucker."

"Of course she does," Tina replied. "The last time I saw her, she was on the business end of a crossbow and I was running for my life."

Interestingly, Ani blushed. Sinclair, who'd been holding my shoulder while he wiped all the holy water off my face, suddenly tightened his grip and I yelped. "Don't start, don't start again!" I yelled, waving my arms frantically. "Let's sit down and talk about this like civilized people!"

"Why?" he asked coldly.

"Uh . . . because I asked nicely?"

He stared at his handkerchief which, now that it wasn't touching me, was starting to smolder. So, once holy water was, like, off my person, it could hurt a vampire? Weird! He tossed it in the wastebasket and scowled at the Blond Warriors.

"As my queen commands," he managed to spit out through gritted teeth, to my surprise and everyone else's relief.

Chapter 15

"YOU guys get that you're just a loaded gun someone else is aiming. A tool, a big, dumb, tool." Jessica popped another cracker into her mouth, chewed, then added, "You get that, right?"

"That's not true," Wild Bill whined.

"Sure it is. You guys weren't even a team before the Puppet Master came along. Now you're running around staking dead people. And you don't even know why."

Sinclair nodded approvingly and sipped his Earl Grey. The vampires were comfortably spread out on one side of the table, and everybody else was crammed together on the other side. Father Markus had hung his crucifix around his neck, keeping it in plain sight, which made the other vamps a little antsy. They kept trying to look at him, and then their gaze would skitter away.

Across the table, the others jumped a foot whenever Tina or Sinclair reached for more tea. It was kind of funny.

"So who *is* the Puppet Master?" Tina asked. "Don't any of you have any idea?"

"No," Ani replied.

"Oh, come now."

"I swear! Everything's been anonymous. We assumed it was some rich vampire victim. You know, someone who lost a loved one to . . . to one of you."

"Ennnnhhhhh! Thanks for playing . . . what do we have for her, Johnny?"

"Quit doing your game show host schtick, Marc," I ordered. "You're confusing the vampires. They're not big TV watchers."

"Certainly not daytime television," Sinclair sniffed.

Marc smirked. "My point is, I doubt it. Remember, guys, we were talking about how it had to be a vampire, because he knew who was dead and who wasn't? How would a regular person know that? It's not like Eric keeps a list . . . oh, John Smith rose from the dead, better write that down."

"No," Sinclair said, and he was actually smiling. Thank God. "I don't have a list."

"Actually, *I* was saying that," Jessica said, "and you're right. The bad guy's one of you," she said, pointing to the vampire half of the tea table. In fact, she was pointing right at me, and I batted her hand away. "You've got to figure out who, and why. And ouch, not so hard, Bets."

"Sorry. I get nervous when people make announcements about killers and then point at me. So, why? Why would a vampire want to kill other vampires?"

"If we knew the why, we'd know the who," Tina said, sounding like an undead Dr. Seuss.

"You at least know where your funding comes from," Sinclair said. It wasn't a question.

"All funds required for our activities are wired from a Swiss bank account," Father Markus explained.

"Ah, the Swiss," Tina muttered. "Accommodating financiers to Nazis, third-world dictators, and vampire killers."

Nobody said anything to that.

Father Markus cleared his throat. "All our instructions and intel arrive via anonymous e-mails."

"Intel?" I smirked. Someone's been watching too many *Alias* reruns.

"Devo is our computer expert, but even he has been unable to trace the e-mails."

"Oh, you bothered to try?" Sinclair asked politely. Even seated, he dwarfed everyone at the table. "I thought you had just taken your marching orders and off you went like good little meat puppets."

"Sinclair!" I gasped. Meat puppets? Where had he picked *that* up?

"So who's a suspect?" Jessica asked quickly. She got up to pace, which was always annoying; but she'd been doing it for fifteen years and wasn't likely to stop now. "I mean, assuming you guys are interested in finding out."

"Of course we are," Father Markus said, offended.

"Why?" Tina challenged. "We're still vampires. You're still our food."

"I am not, young lady," Father Markus said sternly, which was a laugh, because Tina had about ninety years on him. "And it's one thing to assume you're doing the Lord's work, and another to find out you're being used and you don't know why, or by whom."

Tina actually looked chastened; Sinclair mostly looked amused.

"What, find out?" Marc shook his head. "You always knew you were being used. You just didn't care until an upstanding citizen pointed it out."

Father Markus shrugged, but his color was high, like he was embarrassed but didn't want to say anything else.

"So, we think it's a vampire," Jessica said, crunching crumbs into the carpet as she got up to pace. *Dammit!* "Well, there's a pretty good suspect right here in this room."

"Who?" I asked, surprised.

"Me," Sinclair said.

"Well, if you've been sending us all that money," Ani said sweetly, "thanks."

"Oh, come on. Sinclair the Puppet Master? Well, okay, *that* makes sense, but he wouldn't kill vampires. Right? Right."

"Why not?" Marc asked. "No offense, Sinclair, but you're not exactly the type to enjoy competition."

"You are a keen observer, Dr. Spangler."

Marc glowed under the sarcastic praise. *I* wanted to know how Sinclair knew Marc's last name . . . I'd never told him.

"And now that Nostro's dead," Marc continued, like a gay, male, younger version of that old lady from *Murder, She Wrote,* "you can thin the herd a little more. And you can sure afford to finance the Blade Warriors."

"That's ridiculous!" I said hotly. "He's a loathsome crumb and an overbearing control freak, but he wouldn't start slaughtering his own people."

"Thank you, Elizabeth," he said politely.

"Well, he might," Tina said with her trademark ruthless honesty, "but he'd do it himself. He wouldn't farm the work out to a bunch of pimply . . . um, to other people."

"Also," Sinclair added quietly, "I would never harm the queen."

I grinned in spite of myself. He likes me, he really really likes me!

"Then there's you, Bets," Jessica said, and my grin fell off my face. "It's pretty well known you hate being the queen, and that you can't stand most vampires. Plus, you're not exactly the type to get your hands dirty. It'd be just like you to hire a group to do the work for you."

I wanted to say something like, "Knock it off!" or "Drop dead!" But nothing she had said was untrue. So I just drank tea and glared.

"Except she has no interest—or participation—in

vampire politics. And she wouldn't know who was a vampire and who wasn't. Not to mention, she doesn't have the money to fund this operation. Which brings us," Sinclair added lazily, "to you, Jessica."

"Oh, come on!" I yelled.

But Jess was unfazed. "True, I'm a pretty good suspect." She started ticking the reasons off on her long fingers. "I've got the money. I'm sympathetic to my friend's plight—namely, that she doesn't want to be queen of the vamps. I don't much give a crap if vampires get killed or not—sorry, guys. I'm rich enough to be able to hide my tracks. Except there's one problem."

"She isn't the one," Father Markus said.

"No?" Jessica smiled.

"No," he said firmly. "I've known your family since you were small, Miss Watkins. It's not in you."

"You knew my father, right?" she said, hanging onto her smile.

"I did. It's not in *you*," he repeated stubbornly.

"Hello?" a voice said, and then Monique stuck her head through the doorway. Tina and Sinclair didn't move, but the rest of us jumped a foot. "Did I miss anything?"

"Who is *that?*" Jon slobbered.

"Never you mind. What are you doing here, Monique?"

"Nobody was at the hotel, so I made an educated guess. What's going on? My, what a beautiful room." She settled herself between Tina and me, looking adorable in beige capris and a red sleeveless sweater.

"We're trying to figure out who the Puppet Master is," I explained. "Um, Monique, you're not rich, are you?"

She was pouring herself a cup of tea, and didn't spill a drop. "Oh, good gosh no," she said mildly. "Not compared to some." She raised her eyebrows and nodded at Sinclair and Jessica.

"And what of the good Detective Berry?" Sinclair asked.

"What, Nick?" I was totally surprised. He wouldn't have occurred to me in a million years.

"Isn't it true that he's reappeared in your life after a three month absence? And as a member of the police force, he has access to information the rest of us can only dream of."

"Yeah, but . . . he's so nice."

"He didn't look terribly nice when he was drooling and cringing and crawling around your carpet last spring," Tina said frankly.

"But he doesn't remember any of that!"

"Doesn't he?"

I fell silent; I had no idea what Nick remembered.

"After his experience with us, he has good reason to hate vampires," Sinclair added.

"The trouble is," Tina said, "we have too many suspects. It could be any one of Nostro's followers. Betsy isn't exactly . . . ah . . . acknowledged by all of us as the rightful queen."

"Mongrels," Monique said under her breath.

"Some vampires might perceive that as a chance to seize power," Tina continued.

"Which eliminates the number of suspects to about three hundred," I said glumly.

"More like two hundred thousand," Sinclair corrected.

"That's how many vampires are running around on the planet?" Ani asked, looking appalled.

"Give or take a few hundred."

We batted the subject around a while longer, but soon enough it was close to four in the morning and we decided to call it quits. Also, we were out of tea and the rest of the cookies were squashed.

Tina and Sinclair left first, giving the Blade Warriors their backs, which was a major diss, but I kind of liked them for it. I wanted to know how they'd known to come back earlier tonight. I started to follow them out when Ani grabbed my arm.

"Uh . . . Betsy . . . Betsy's okay, right?"

"It's my name," I said, puzzled, as Marc and Jessica filed past us, arguing, as usual.

"I was . . . uh . . . I was wondering about Tina."

"Tina?"

"Short, good legs, blond hair, big pretty eyes—Tina."

"Oh," I said, catching on, "*that* Tina. What about her?"

"What's her, you know, her situation?" Ani was practically jumping from one foot to the other—I wondered if she'd had too much tea. "Is she with that Sinclair guy?"

"Uh, no." *I am. Sort of.*

"So what's her story?"

"She's a hundred-year-old vampire who could eat you for breakfast before snapping your spine like a drumstick," I said, deciding to nip this in the bud right now. "She's loyal to Sinclair, fierce as shit, stubborn as hell, and a killer on a liquid diet. That's her story."

"Right, but is she seeing anyone?"

"Ani, you're a vampire killer!"

"Well, you guys have spent the whole night explaining that some of you are good," she snapped back. "You're the furthest thing from a vampire I've ever seen. You're like those cheerleaders I went to high school with. I think in the interest of live-to-undead personal relations—"

"Oh, ick. Go away. No, she's not seeing anyone. But being that the last time you two met, you tried to cut her head off, I foresee problems in this burgeoning relationship—*aagghh!*"

Tina had stuck her head through the door. Dammit! I was tying bells to her *and* Sinclair. "Ani, dear, you left your headlights on," she said. "I thought you might like to know."

"Thanks!" she said, leaping past me and practically knocking me into the table. "I'll take care of that right now. And I . . . I've been meaning to talk to you. To . . . um . . . apologize for trying to kill you and everything."

"That's all right, dear. You didn't know any better."

"Right! That's exactly right! I thought all blood suckers were heartless killers, but I see now that maybe I was wrong." The door slammed behind them, but I could still hear Ani. "Maybe we could talk it over a cup of coffee or something . . . sometime . . ."

"Ick," I said again, but who was paying attention? Nobody.

Chapter 16

I opened my eyes to see Marie hovering over me.

"You've got to stop doing that," I said, throwing back my comforter with a groan.

"I'm bored."

"Well, sugar, what the hell am I supposed to do about it? Go find your dad."

"And you never wake up when I talk to you."

"Never mind about that." I yawned. Another night in the salt mines. "Scoot, I've got to get dressed for work."

I jumped in the shower, got cleaned up, and dressed for work. Marie had indeed scooted, and for a change I had my bedroom to myself.

Jessica tapped on the door while I was putting on my mascara, and I yelled for her to come in.

"Evening, dead girl. Um. Why are your books all facing the wrong way?"

I shrugged.

"Fine, be mysterious. Sinclair called. He's bringing some people over tonight."

"That's nice. I'm not going to be here, though."

"Ooooh, the diss *du jour*."

"It's not a diss; I've got to work. Besides, it serves him right for not even asking if he can come over."

"Yeah, that'll learn him. Listen, are you going to keep an eye on the Blade Warriors, or what?"

"Me?" I said, appalled. And what was I thinking when I bought navy blue mascara? The new black, my foot. My eyelashes looked cyanotic. "Why the hell would I do that?"

"Well, you want to make sure they're not going to run around axing any more vamps, right?"

"Why would they? We explained all that last night. About how they're toys in the hands of a fiendish master, blah-blah, time to stop killing dead people and figure out what's going on."

"I still think someone should keep an eye on them."

"*You* watch the zit brigade."

"Oh, that's nice," she said, but she laughed.

"Not a single one of them can walk into a bar and legally order a drink. I didn't like hanging around with teenagers when I *was* one."

"Says the former Miss Burnsville."

"I can't help it," I said with great dignity, "if my fellow inmates liked me more than I liked them."

"Maybe you can channel the Warriors' energy in a new direction," she suggested.

I nearly put my eye out with the mascara wand. "Maybe *you* can, you're so worried about it. I'm in charge of the dead people, not the live ones."

"Well, I think they're looking for direction." She added slyly, "Jon's already called for you five times."

"What, during the day? Idiot."

"I think he's got a crush."

"So that's where you're going with this. Great. Just what I need."

"Hey, there's worse problems to have."

"Name one."

"I can't right now. But I'm sure something will come to me," she added cheerfully.

I was in a fairly foul temper when I stomped out of the house. Unfortunately, I wasn't quite quick enough. I ran into Sinclair, Tina, Monique, and a vampire I didn't know on my way to the car.

"How nice of you to come out to meet us," Sinclair said. "Are you feeling all right?"

"I'm on my way to work." I glanced at my watch. "In fact, I've got about twenty minutes to get there. Bye."

"This is Sarah," he continued as if I hadn't spoken. "Sarah, this is Elizabeth the First, our sovereign."

The First? I was a First?

Sarah nodded coolly. She was short, about Tina's height, with close-cropped brown hair and brown eyes with green flecks. She was wearing black slacks, a sleeveless black turtleneck, and crocodile flats. Her slacks were belted, also via crocodile. Sharp!

"Sarah's in town to pay her respects," Tina said, breaching the silence.

"Hardly," Sarah sniffed. Tina jabbed her in the side with her elbow, but Sarah's expression didn't change.

"Nice to meet you," I said, trying to lighten the tension. One thing about dead people, once they'd been vampires for a few decades, they really figured out the style thing. "Great shoes."

"You killed Nostro." It wasn't a question.

"Well, yes."

"*You* did."

"Sarah . . ." Sinclair warned.

"Hey, it was self-defense! Sort of. Okay, not really. I mean, it was self-defense in the sense that he eventually would have tried to kill me again, and he'd already tried to kill me twice—or was it three times?—and I sort of caught him between attempts, but it's not like I started anything. *He* started it! And I didn't exactly do the deed myself, you know. I mean, I was responsible and all, because I set the Fiends on him, but I didn't actually bite his head off."

Sarah was staring at me. Tina was staring at the ground and nibbling on her lower lip, and Sinclair had his eyes closed.

"What?" I griped. "I'm just telling her what happened. And now I really, really have to go. Go in if you want, Jessica's home, but next time call first so I can be home when you come over." Ha! Not likely. But it was the polite thing to say.

"I'm not going in that house," Sarah said.

"What have you got against my house? Are you the one Tina and Monique tried to bring over the other night, but you got pissy and walked away?"

"I did not get pissy."

"Okay, whatever." God, what a weirdo! "Never mind, I don't want to know. Listen, I'm going to be late."

"So you keep saying," Tina teased, "but I notice you're not going anywhere."

"We have pressing business," Sinclair-the-killjoy reminded me.

"Give me a break. You guys don't need me to figure out who the Puppet Master is. Go talk to the Warriors some more."

"Actually, they're meeting us here." He whipped out a card. From where, I had no idea—he wasn't wearing a suit jacket and his shirt didn't have any pockets. "We made the arrangements last night, and Jon gave me this."

"They've got business cards?" I rolled my eyes. "Jesus, why am I not surprised?" They all flinched. "And will you guys stop jumping like you've been goosed every time I take the Lord's name in vain?"

"Some things you cannot order," Sarah said, still ice-cool.

"Yeah, well, okay. Bye."

I walked past them and felt their eyeballs on me all the way to my car. Which was just as unpleasant as it sounds.

* * *

"YOU don't want that one," I whispered. "They say it's hand-stitched, but they lie."

"Oh-ho," my would-be shoe buyer said. "Tricky tricky."

"You might try one of the Pradas," I suggested. "I know she's really ubiquitous, but she deserves it. Look at the design! It's like a kimono for your foot."

"It's nice, but—"

"Holy God, it's true. You really do work at Macy's!"

I turned. Jon, weirdo leader of the Blind Warriors and surfing beach escapee, was standing by the cash register, staring at me with his mouth open so wide, I could see his fillings.

"What?" I snapped. Then, mindful of my customer, I forced a smile. "I'll be with you in a minute."

"No rush. I've got plenty of shoes," he retorted, grinning.

I turned back to my customer, who was determinedly jamming a size seven Escada onto her size nine foot. "Stop that," I said. "You'll ruin the lacing. Let me get you one in your size."

"This-is-my-size," she puffed.

Fine, enjoy blisters the size of plums. "I'll be over here if you need me," I said sweetly, then seized Jon by the elbow and hustled him over by the boots. He yelped as his feet left the floor. I put him down and hissed in his ear, "What are you doing here?"

"Wanted to see if it was true," he whispered back, his breath tickling my ear. "Are you sure you're a vampire?"

"You would not believe how many people ask me that."

"I'll bet," he said, staring at my name tag.

"What do you want?"

"Are you going to eat your customer?"

"No!"

"Don't yell, I was just asking. Can't we all just get along?"

"Says the vampire killer."

"I've reformed," he said, sounding hurt.

"Hmmm."

"Why are you wearing sunglasses inside at night?"

"Because I'm a big Corey Hart fan?" I guessed.

His blank stare reminded me that I was dating myself. Obviously the boy wasn't up on his '80s pop. "Never mind. Did Sinclair put you up to this? Oh, God—he's not here, is he?" I looked around wildly, but only saw retail customers.

"Is he your boyfriend?"

"Are you in law school? What's with the twenty questions? And no, he is not."

"Because he sort of acts like he is."

"One of the many, many reasons why I despise him. Now will you take a hike? You should be meeting with Sinclair and Tina and figuring out who sent you out to kill us, not bugging me."

He shifted from one foot to another. "Well . . . Ani's there, she's the brains, not me."

"Ani, the brains?"

"So I figured I'd come and see you. But if you really want me to go."

"Finally, he catches on! Yes, I really want you to go. Thanks a ton for stopping by," I said, giving him a gentle shove in the direction of the exit. "Bye!"

He turned and started walking backward, his hands stuffed in his faded jeans which were, I might add, about three sizes too small. His blond hair gleamed under the fluorescent lights, and even from eight feet away I could see how blue his eyes were, and how well he filled out his T-shirt. He practically radiated Good Boy Vibe. "I'm sorry I tried to kill you," he called, still walking backward.

I mimed locking my lips shut and throwing the key over my shoulder. He flashed another grin—product of a really excellent dental plan—turned around, and left in the direction of Orange Julius.

Nice kid. If Jessica was right, and he did have the hots for me, I'd have to squash him gently. For one thing, he was ten years younger. For another, he was alive. For another, I was a vampire and he was a vampire killer.

Besides, between work, and the queen of the dead thing, and fending off Sinclair, I just didn't have time to cram a boyfriend into my schedule.

Too bad.

Chapter 17

MY cell phone rang while I was on 494 West. I kept forgetting to change the tones, so it burbled "Funkytown" at me when it rang.

"Hello?"

"Hey, where are you?" Jessica. "I'm entertaining Sinclair and Tina all night, here."

"I care! It's their own fault for not calling ahead. I'm on my way to check on the Fiends."

"Ooooh, cool. When are you going to bring me to meet them?"

"Never."

"Oh, come on!" she whined.

"Forget it. They're too dangerous."

"You say that about all the fun stuff," she pouted.

"Oh, yeah, real fun. Crazed bloodsuckers who are more animal than human. Hey, trust me on this, if they weren't my responsibility, I wouldn't go near them."

"Fine, fine. Catch you later."

"Give Sinclair a smack for me." I disconnected and tossed my phone onto the seat beside me. It was too bad I couldn't grant her request, but I wasn't about to take chances with her life. Even if she did have my car windows fixed while I was sleeping.

I pulled up to Nostro's house. He'd made the Fiends, as a sort of twisted experiment, and we still kept them at his house. Why not? He sure didn't need it anymore.

The Fiends were what happened when you didn't let a newborn vampire feed. They went out of their minds with hunger and lost most of their I.Q. Not to mention their ability to walk on two legs and bathe regularly. It was disgusting and sad at the same time.

I went around to the barn in the back—probably the only barn in Minnetonka—and observed the Fiends gamboling in the moonlight like big undead puppies. They rushed over to me when they smelled me and I patted a couple of them, feeling stupid. They had once been human, and I felt ridiculous treating them like pets. Of course, they acted like pets—hideously dangerous, unstable, bloodthirsty pets—but never mind.

"Majesty!"

Alice hailed me and hurried across the wide yard. She'd been about fourteen when Nostro had turned her, the big jerk. Perpetually in the throes of adolescence! Talk about your fate worse than death.

"Hi, Alice." She was looking especially cute in a blue jumper and a white blouse. Her curly red hair was caught back in a blue headband. Bare feet. Toenails painted sky blue. "How's it going?"

"Fine, Majesty."

"For the millionth time: Betsy."

"They seem happy to see you," she said, avoiding the whole name issue.

"Yeah. They look good. You're doing a great job."

Alice glowed. Or maybe it was because she'd recently fed; her cheeks were positively rosy. As for the Fiends, they drank pigs' blood, and the weekly butcher's bill was high indeed. This was extremely weird, as every vampire I'd ever met, including me, needed "live" blood.

Maybe because the Fiends were barely human, so to speak, they didn't have to have the stuff right from the source.

"I think they're getting better," Alice said. "I left them some books and they didn't shit all over them this time. They did nibble on them, though."

"I don't need to hear this. But thanks anyway. How are you doing?"

"Oh, well, you know," she said demurely. She gestured at the giant, empty house. "It's a little lonely out here once in a while, but Tina keeps me company."

"Well, jeez, Alice, you're not a prisoner. You can leave whenever you want. You don't have to live out here."

"This is my job now," she said seriously. "It's the most important thing there is."

"That's the spirit." I guess. "Uh . . . thanks again."

"I'm here to serve, Majesty."

"Cut that out. You have everything you need here?"

"Yes, of course," she said cheerfully.

It didn't look like it to me, but I suppose after living under Nostro's regime, playing zookeeper to a bunch of feral vampires was a walk in the park. Me, I'd have been bored out of my mind by now. But Alice never complained, and when I made noises about getting another vampire to take over Fiend duty, to give her a break, she practically cried.

"Well, I'll be out next week. You've got my cell. Call if you need anything."

"I certainly will, Majesty."

I sighed. "And work on the Betsy thing, will you?"

She just smiled.

"They should all be staked."

"Jesus!" I nearly jumped into Alice's arms. She put out a hand to steady me and then, as if afraid of touching my exalted self, pulled back. "Sinclair, I swear to God, if you don't stop doing that . . ." In the moonlight he looked like a moody devil.

"Majesty," Alice said, tipping her head deferentially.

"Alice," His Majesty said.

"What the hell are you doing here?" I asked, undeferentially.

He shrugged.

"Well, that was helpful. I was just about to leave. Don't be staking the Fiends after I go."

"I'll come with you."

Great. Why was that thought equally thrilling and annoying? "See you, Alice."

"Majesties."

"Good night, Alice."

The Fiends whined when I left, but then I heard a splash and heard slurping—*yeerrgghh!* Feeding time at the zoo. I hoped Alice hadn't gotten her jumper all bloody.

Sinclair caught my hand and held it as we walked back to the cars. Awwww, just like an undead couple going steady! "There's been another killing," he said.

I nearly tripped over a gopher hole. "What? When? Why didn't you say anything a minute ago?"

"Tina and I think it's best to keep it from the other vampires until we find the culprit."

"Oh." Too bad they hadn't kept it from *me*. "Anybody we know?"

"No. A woman named Jennifer. Rather young for a vampire, in fact, Tina found her death certificate and it was less than twenty years old."

"A mere infant. Huh, that's weird. Jon didn't say a word tonight about killing somebody else. I'll strangle the little creep!"

Sinclair's grip tightened, ever so slightly. "You saw Jon tonight?"

"Yeah, he came to bug me at work."

"I'll speak to him about that."

"You will not," I said, irritated. "What, you're the

only one allowed to bug me at work? And let go of my hand."

"Yes. And no."

"We're getting off the subject."

"A hazard in any conversation with you. But you're quite right. Jon and Ani swear they had nothing to do with it."

"You think they're on the up and up?"

"Yes. Tina concurs. Also, she was with Ani most of the evening."

"That's never going to work, FYI," I predicted. "Ani won't be Tina's pet, and you can't tell me Tina's looking for a girlfriend."

"I can't?"

"Plus, hello, they have *nothing* in common. Not to mention the age difference. The *hundred-year* age difference."

"I don't know that an age difference is so insurmountable," he said carefully, then added, "It's really none of our business."

"Oh, shut up. And let go of my hand!"

"I decline. Stop squirming. At any rate, this Jennifer is dead. Someone is still killing."

I kicked at a tuft of grass, which went flying like a divot on a golf course. "Well, at least the kids didn't screw us over. So now what?"

"Now we must examine the body. Maybe we'll find something we missed before."

I stopped short. Sinclair kept going, so I was nearly yanked off my feet. "Nuh-uh, count me out! *So* not on my to-do list for the night!"

"It's your responsibility," he said implacably.

"Forget it! Seriously, Eric, dead bodies creep me out. I can't even watch *Night of the Living Dead* by myself."

He rubbed his forehead as if a killer migraine had sprouted. "Elizabeth . . ."

"You're not really going to wreck my evening like this, are you?" I begged. "I just can't think of anything worse."

He laughed. "Sometimes . . . frequently . . . you're too adorable."

"Now who's getting off the subject? Like I haven't noticed you've led me to your car and are stuffing me—watch the hair!" I warned as he put his hand on my head and tucked me into the passenger side of his Lexus. "Dammit, Sinclair, this isn't over!"

"You can finish it," he said, climbing into the driver's seat, "on the way to the morgue."

FOR that extra creepy touch, the morgue was—get this—in my basement. That's right: *my* basement.

"Just kill me now," I muttered as we descended the stairs.

"Well, where else should we keep the body?" Marc asked, reasonably enough. He'd been key in the evening's body-snatching activities—people hardly ever questioned a doctor's movements. "The Marquette Hotel?"

"Anywhere but our damned house!"

"Oh, you're always complaining."

"Since April," I said darkly, "I've had a lot to complain about."

Marc pondered that one, then finally said, "True enough."

There was quite the party in the basement, though it took a while to find them—the basement ran the length of the house. There was a room on the far end that I'd never been in before, and that's where Tina, Monique, Sarah-the-weirdo, Ani, Jon, and Jessica were waiting for us. Oh, and the dead body. Can't forget that.

"I object again," Sarah said by way of greeting.

"Be quiet," Sinclair ordered.

"What is your problem with our house?" I asked, puzzled. "I mean, I get that you don't like me, if you were fond of Nostro, which calls your taste into severe question, by the way. But what have you got against my digs?"

"I used to work here," she said distantly. "I didn't like it then, and I certainly don't care to be here now."

"Well, sor*ry*! Nobody's making you stay."

"Untrue," Sinclair said, fixing Sarah with his dark gaze. She instantly stopped bitching and stared at the floor.

I wondered what the big deal was. Then it hit me: Sarah didn't like me, wasn't crazy about the fact that I'd killed Nostro, and had recently blown into town. If she had money, that made her a pretty good suspect. No wonder Sinclair wanted to keep her close.

Sarah looked up and said, "Nostro made me."

"Oh." Well, that explained it. He'd been an utter

shit, but his vampires were weirdly loyal, especially the ones he made himself. It made zero sense to me, but what did I know about vamp politics? Nada.

"I had no real love for him," she was saying, "but he deserved my loyalty. He gave me immortality. He made me a goddess among men."

"And a weirdo among the rest of us." Her little revelation had just put her at the top spot of our list of suspects. I wonder if she knew? "Well, we'll just have to agree to disagree, I s'pose."

"I rather doubt that."

"Thank you all for coming," Tina said, cutting Sarah off as she opened her mouth again. "Especially on such a grim errand."

"I told you we needed a big house," Jessica whispered in my ear.

"Yeah, but . . . for this?"

I stepped closer. The dead vampire, Jennifer, was stretched out on the beat-up wooden table in the center of the room. In two pieces.

I gagged and turned my face away. I felt Sinclair rub my back and, weirdly, I took strength from that, and after a minute I was able to look. I wasn't the only one affected. Jessica was so pale she was more gray than brown, and Tina's big eyes were pools of sadness.

"Before you ask," Jon said, looking annoyingly unmoved, "we didn't cut off her head."

"If I thought you had," Sinclair said pleasantly, "there'd be another body here in two pieces."

"Don't start, you guys," I said automatically, as

Jon paled and twitched toward his knife. "Don't you guys have *any* ideas? Anything at all?"

"This is the first killing that didn't happen on a Wednesday," Tina said.

"We always got together on Wednesdays," Ani said. She was walking around the table, inspecting poor headless Jennifer. "It was the only day all our work schedules lined up."

"Ah-ha!" I said. "See, that was my theory all along. Remember, the night Tina and Monique got attacked?"

"Yes, yes, you're very clever," Sinclair said absently. He was prowling right behind Ani, also looking at the body.

"Don't tell me," I said to Jon. "Radio Shack."

"How'd you know?"

"Just a wild guess, Geek Boy. And what the hell's a Devo?"

"He's our computer expert. He—"

"She's been shot," Sinclair said.

"*And* beheaded? Talk about overkill," Jessica muttered. I shuddered.

"With vampires, it's best to be sure," Ani said, almost apologetically.

"Which reminds me," Tina said. "The bullet one of you shot into Her Majesty the Queen. It was a hollow point filled with holy water."

"No wonder it stung like crazy," I commented.

"And you *survived?*" Monique practically gasped. "I can't believe it!"

"Oh, well, you know," I said modestly. Monique

was looking at me with total admiration, which was a pleasant change. Most vampires looked at me like I was a bug.

"Yes, our Elizabeth is just full of surprises," Sinclair said, ruining the moment with his sarcasm. "Which one of you Warriors thought up that charming little gift?"

After a moment's hesitation, Ani slowly raised her hand. She blushed as Tina looked at her reproachfully.

"Hmmm."

"Come on, take it easy on her," Marc said. "You have to admit, it's sort of brilliant."

"Yes, we have to admit that," Tina agreed. "I'll see if the bullets are still in the body. And if they're the same kind, we'll know that the Puppet Master—for want of a better phrase—killed Jennifer. Which is interesting."

I raised my hand. "Um, why?" It was much more gross than interesting, if you asked me. Which nobody had.

"Because we've—the Blade Warriors—agreed to stop killing vampires until we figure out who's been pulling our strings," Jon cut in. "I mean, we all talked last night, after we met you guys—"

"And had tea with us," I said with a triumphant look at Sinclair.

"—and decided to hold off for a while."

"For a while?" Tina and Sinclair asked in unison, equally sharply.

Jon ignored them. "We sent our boss an e-mail

last night. But it looks like he's still killing vampires. Or he's found someone else to do it." He spread his hands, puzzled. "Well, how come? Is he targeting specific vampires, or is he an undead serial killer, or what? I mean, he had to go out and stake this vamp the minute he got our e-mail. Why?"

"If it's even a he," Monique piped up.

"Good point, uh—"

"Monique."

Jon could hardly take his eyes off her, which wasn't surprising. She was really beautiful, and dressed to kill in an Ann Taylor suit, black stockings, and black pumps. Her hair was almost silver against the black of the suit.

Frankly, I had met very few ugly vampires. One, to be exact. And he was more unwashed than unattractive.

Which made sense—every vampire I'd met had been a murder victim, killed by another vampire. And vampires seemed to seek out good-looking people to snack on. I guess because drinking blood seemed so sexual . . . most people wanted to boink good-looking partners. And most vampires wanted to drink from cuties.

Monique was gorgeous, there just wasn't any two ways about it. Tina wasn't exactly hard on the eyes, either. I could see that even Jennifer had been beautiful, though her long, brown hair was matted with blood, and—

"Wait a minute. Don't talk, don't talk!" I clutched my head and writhed.

"What the hell's wrong with you?" Marc asked.

"I know that look," Jessica said. "She's got an idea. Or she needs an Ex-Lax."

"Am I the only one who noticed that all the murder victims are women?" I cried. "Say it isn't so!"

Tina looked startled. "Well . . . yes, I suppose so. That's another thing they all had in common, besides taking place on Wednesdays, and—"

"Don't you guys think that's a little weird?" I asked Tina and Sinclair. Then I rounded on Jon and Ani. "Don't *you* guys?"

"It—uh—didn't make much difference to us," Ani coughed. "We figured you were all bad."

"We're feminists," Jon said, totally straight-faced. "Killing female vamps didn't bother us at all."

"This could shed light on the motive," Sinclair said.

"Ya think?" I asked sarcastically.

"The women all look different, right?" Jessica asked. "So it's not like the killer's going after a certain type. I mean, if he targeted Betsy *and* Tina *and* Monique . . . you three don't look a thing alike. You're not even the same build."

Meaning I'm a disgusting hulk who towers over the delicately built Tina and Monique . . . thanks.

"It's getting kind of late," Monique said after a long silence in which I contemplated my enormous bulk and the others contemplated who-knew-what. "Maybe we could pick this up tomorrow night?"

I had just gotten there, but I wasn't going to argue. Unfortunately, Monique's suggestion meant three nights in a row with these killjoys, trying to solve murders. I stifled the urge to remind them I was a former secretary, not a former homicide detective.

"Does someone have a knife?" Tina asked. "I'd like to see if I can get one of the bullets out."

"Oh, I'm so out of here," I said, turning away. Last straw, last straw! Overload! "Tina, you seriously need a hobby."

"Right now," she said grimly, "my hobby is catching whoever is doing this. I'll take up sewing later."

"I'm holding you to that," I muttered.

Sinclair handed her a pocket knife, which she unfolded with a loud *click.* The blade was almost four inches long—Sinclair was clearly a big believer in the Boy Scouts' Motto. Tina bent over Jennifer's body and started probing at her chest.

I practically ran up the stairs.

Chapter 18

JON followed me all the way up to my bedroom. "You know," he said, stiff-arming the door open when I tried to close it on him, "I'm the one who talked the Warriors into backing off you guys."

"That's super. Your good citizenship medal is in the mail. Why don't you go home and wait for it?"

"It's just that after meeting you it didn't seem right."

"Okey-dokey. 'Night!"

"Yeah, um, listen, you don't need to bite anyone or anything, do you?" He sounded weirdly hopeful; I almost hated to tell him I didn't. And what kind of behavior was this for a vampire killer? "Did anybody ever tell you, you've got the prettiest green eyes?"

"They're not green; they're mold colored. Jon, I'm trying to get ready for bed, here," I said, trying to keep the exasperation out of my voice. "When the sun comes up, if I'm not in bed I'll keel over wherever I'm standing."

"Really? Like, no matter what you're doing, you'll just fall down asleep? Like, totally helpless and all?"

"It's not as exciting as it sounds." I put my hand on his face and gently shoved him backward. "So, good night."

"I'll see you tomorrow," he began, and then he was suddenly jerked out of sight. Then Sinclair was shouldering his way past me and kicking the door shut behind him.

"For crying out loud," I started in, "when did my bedroom become Grand Goddamned Central?"

Sinclair leaned against the door and crossed his arms over his chest. "I insist you discourage that infant immediately."

"In case you weren't paying attention, I *have* been. It's not my fault he's interested in vampires."

Sinclair snorted. "He is not. He's interested in you."

"Well, what am I supposed to do about it?" I bitched. "I've got enough problems right now."

"Problems, coupled with the prettiest green eyes," he said dryly.

"Eavesdropper! Go away, I have to get ready for bed."

"You're not going to wear those silly sushi-print pajamas, are you?"

"Hey, they're comfy. Go away."

"Remind me to buy you some decent night attire."

"I'm having bomb dogs sniff over anything you buy me." I tugged at the door knob, but he wouldn't budge. I slapped at his shoulder. "Will you get out of here? Don't you have to get back to the Marquette before you burst into flames?"

"Oh, I don't know," he replied casually. "There's plenty of room here. I thought I might stay."

I knew it, I *knew* living in a mansion was a bad idea. There was no graceful excuse to get out of having an overnight guest.

"Fine, whatever, but you're not sleeping in here."

"No?"

"No!"

"I'll go back to the Marquette," he suggested, "for a kiss."

"Fine, *fine*, jeez, you're so annoying." I snatched handfuls of his hair, jerked his face down to mine, kissed him on the bridge of the nose, and let go. He tried to grab me, but I was wise to his ways, and dodged his hands. "Now go away. Deal's a deal."

"Hmph." But he left. Thank goodness! I think.

I woke up the next night and laid there for a minute, feeling anxious but not sure why. Then I remembered: murders, playing detective, Jon and Sinclair. And that was just the stuff on the top of my brain.

Marie was sitting in the chair beside my bed, looking reproachful.

"What?" I asked.

"You used to be around here a lot more," she said wistfully.

"Sorry, sunshine. There's stuff going on . . . never mind." I wasn't going to talk about beheadings with a kindergartener. Instead, I sat up and swung my legs over the side of the bed. "You see anything wrong with these pajamas?"

"No. I like them."

"Exactly!" Stupid Sinclair. "Well, I have some stuff to do tonight, but maybe tomorrow we could—ow!" I'd tripped climbing off my bed (it was the size of a train car) and fell into Marie.

Actually, I fell *through* Marie. It was like plunging into a lake in February. I hit the carpet with a thump and could see her little feet, sticking through my arm.

"Jesus Christ," I said, and it was a good thing I didn't need to breathe, because right now I was breathless.

"Don't be mad," Marie said anxiously. "I didn't want to tell you."

"Oh my *God*. You're . . . you . . ." I waved my hand through her head. Holy shit on toast! There was a ghost in my bedroom!

I scrambled to my feet and lunged through my bedroom door, totally ignoring Marie's pleas to come back. Good thing the door was open, or I would have crashed through it. I nearly knocked Jessica down the stairs and went straight out the front door, where I slammed into Sinclair so hard, I bounced off him and lay on the sidewalk like a stunned beetle.

"I thought you were going to get rid of those ridiculous pajamas."

I jumped up and practically climbed him like a tree. "Eric, Eric, the worst, the absolute worst . . . in there . . . in my room . . ." I pointed to the house.

He grabbed my arms. "What's wrong? Are you hurt? Did someone touch you? Is Jon here? I'll pull out his carotid if he—"

"My room . . . in my room . . . up there . . . Marie . . . in my room—"

"Majesty! Calm down. What's wrong?" Tina, running up the sidewalk. They must have just pulled up. Nice! Don't call or anything, you guys. Even in the midst of total panic, I felt annoyed. "Did someone try to kill you again?"

"I wish! In my room, there's a dead girl in my room!"

"There's a dead girl out here," Sinclair said, puzzled.

"Not me, fool!"

"Come on. Show me." He tucked my hand into his and started up the walk.

I yanked on his hand so hard he nearly fell over backward. "No! I can't go back in there, Eric, I can't! I'll go stay with you at the Marquette, okay? Only let's go right now, okay? I'll drive. Let's go! Okay?"

Eric's dark eyebrows shot up so high, I thought they'd leave his forehead. "Well," he said slowly, "if you feel that strongly about it . . ."

"Don't you *dare*," Tina said. "Opportunistic bastard. She doesn't know what she's saying."

"Is that any way to talk to your king?" he asked, sounding wounded.

She snorted. "When the king's acting like an ass, yes. Come on, Majesty. Let's go see your dead girl."

"You guys are insane! I'm not going back in there ever again!"

"What about your shoes?"

Good point. I had to get them out! I didn't know if Marie could slime them with ghostly protoplasm, but I wasn't about to take the chance. "Will you come with me?" I asked, trying not to sound as pathetic as I felt. "Both of you?"

"Yes, of course." Sinclair patted me. Too bad I couldn't work up much mad about it—I had bigger problems. "Don't be frightened. I can hardly believe this is the woman who set the Fiends on Nostro."

"*Totally* different."

"Frankly, I always thought you were too flighty and capricious to ever feel true fear."

I jerked my hand out of his. "Fuck you, too."

"Ah, that's better. The true Queen has rejoined us."

Jessica opened the door, disheveled and annoyed. "You nearly killed me!" she yelled. "What the hell's going on?"

I was shivering like a wet dog. "You won't even believe it."

She followed the three of us up the stairs, bitching nonstop, until I got to my room and rushed through the doorway before I could lose my nerve. Marie was still in her chair, but her lower lip was pooched out and she glared at me.

"There! Dead girl!"

"What are you talking about?" Jessica asked.

Sinclair shook his head. "I don't see anyone, Elizabeth."

I pointed. "But she's *right* there. In the chair by my bed. See?"

They were all staring at me. So was Marie, for that extra creepy touch.

I tried again. "She's right over there. Overalls, headband. Saddle shoes! How can you not see those darling shoes?" I turned to Tina and Sinclair. "You guys see her, right? Super vampire vision, or whatever?"

"No," Tina said apologetically.

"Sure you do. She's right there!"

"I'm sorry, Majesty. No." Then Sinclair, still staring, struck her on the elbow, and her eyes widened. "Yes."

"You guys are nuts," Jessica said. "I'm straining my eyes so hard I've got a headache. There's nothing there."

"There is," Sinclair said. "A girl-child. Blonde. Big eyes. Messy hair."

"Ha! So you *do* see her!"

"We see her," Sinclair said carefully, "because you have willed us to."

Oh, now what bullshit was this? "What are you talking about?"

"You've forced us to see," Tina explained.

"What are you guys talking about?" Jessica practically yelled.

Just then, Marie burst into tears. "Stop it!" she sobbed. "I hate that! I hate when people talk about me like I'm not here!"

"Jeez, hon, don't do that," I said quickly.

"What?" Jessica asked.

"She says she doesn't like it when we talk about her like she's not here."

"Tell her we're sorry," Jessica said, rolling her eyes.

Marie cried harder. "I can hear *you*."

"Jessica, get lost," I snapped. "You're not helping at all."

"Gladly! Hallucinating bloodsuckers I do *not* need. Plus, I missed my nap today and I'm getting sick of these midnight meetings." She stormed out, slamming the door behind her.

"Marie." I was finally starting to calm down. I mean, the kid was dead and all, but she hadn't scared me on purpose. And she was so little. "Marie, why didn't you tell me you were . . . uh . . ."

"Because I knew you'd be like this," she said, still crying.

I couldn't stand it. The poor kid! Dead and stuck in this oversized starter home with *me*. For eternity!

I swiftly crossed the room, knelt, and hugged her. And nearly let go of her. It was like embracing an ice sculpture. But at least I could touch her now. "Don't cry," I said into her teeny, perfect, ghostly ear. "We'll fix it."

She sniffed and hugged me back. Pretty good

grip for a little kid, too. "No you won't. Nobody can."

"We're not like the other people who have lived here," Sinclair commented.

I turned and looked at him, pulling Marie into my lap. "What, you can hear her now?"

"Yes. She was very faint at first, but now I can hear her and see her perfectly well." He was giving me the strangest look. "Thanks to you."

"Oh, stop it. Listen, Marie, is there a reason you're stuck here? Do we need to find your . . . uh . . . bones or something?"

"No."

"It's okay, we don't mind looking."

"The perfect activity for a Sunday night," Sinclair muttered.

I ignored him, warming to my subject. "Yeah, we'll look. Then, when we find your . . . when we find you, we can give you a proper burial, and you can go to Heaven!"

"I'm buried in the front yard," she said. "Under the fence on the left side, by the big elm tree."

I tried not to barf. Bodies of little girls in my front yard! Jesus! "Well . . . uh . . . that's . . ." I was totally at a loss for words.

"Marie," Tina said, squatting until they were eye level, "why are you here, darling?"

"I'm waiting for my mom."

"And when did you . . . when did people stop being able to see you?"

Marie looked confused. "I'm five," she finally said. "I've been five for a long time."

Tina tried again. "What year were you born?"

"My birthday's in April," she said proudly. "That's the diamond month! April tenth, nineteen forty-five."

There was a pause, then Tina said tactfully, "Well . . . sweetie . . . chances are your mother is already dead. Why don't you try to find her? I'm sure she's waiting for you."

"She's not dead," Marie said solemnly, her big teary eyes fixed on Tina's dark gaze.

"How d'you know?" I asked curiously.

"Because I'm still *here*."

"And you've been here . . . all this time?"

She nodded.

"Holy shit," I commented. It was just like that little weirdo in *The Sixth Sense*! I saw dead people!

Now it made sense. The way the house kept changing hands. The owner's desperation to sell. The continually plummeting price. The way Marie wouldn't eat or drink with me. The way she was always around, no matter what time it was. Maybe ordinary humans couldn't see Marie, but some of them must have known something was wrong, because this house had been on the market for ages.

"Can we . . ." I swallowed. "Can we dig you up and put you somewhere else?"

Marie shrugged.

Memo to me: Dig up dead kid ASAP and move her OUT OF FRONT YARD.

"This is all very interesting," Sinclair commented, "and bears further scrutiny, but we have work to do."

"Eric Sinclair, you heartless bastard!" I covered my mouth. "Oh, shit, I shouldn't have said that. Oh, *shit,* I shouldn't have said *that!*"

Marie was giggling through her fingers. "It's all right," she told me. "I know those words. One time when the workmen were fixing the basement and one of them dropped a cement block on his foot—"

"Never mind, I can guess the rest."

"It's not personal, dear," Sinclair told Marie gently. "But we have more time-sensitive matters to attend to."

"Jerkoff," I coughed into my fist.

"She's been here for over half a century," he pointed out. Then he looked directly at Marie. "No one will forget about you."

"It's all right," she said at once. "Betsy can see me. She could always see me. And she can *touch* me. You'll come back, won't you?"

"Bet on it. Besides, I have no choice. I live in this fu— this mausoleum. But *no* creeping around and scaring the crap out of me anymore, agreed?"

"Hmph. Okay."

"It *is* fun to watch her jump," Sinclair told Marie, who laughed again.

"What's the rush?" I asked. "Did somebody else get . . . uh . . . did something else happen?"

"There are a few vampires in town who wish to pay their respects," Tina explained.

"Ugh."

"Sorry. And the bullets I . . . ah . . . found last night did match the ones the kids were using."

"Oh-ho."

"So we have things to discuss."

"Right." I turned to Marie. "Boring grown-up stuff, sorry. But I'll be back."

"I'll be here," she said, without the slightest trace of irony.

Chapter 19

THE berating started as soon as we left the house. "How could it have escaped your notice that Marie was a ghost?" Sinclair asked. "You've lived in this house how many weeks now?"

"Hey, I've had a lot of things on my mind," I said defensively. "What, I'm gonna interrogate a five-year-old? Besides, she never told me."

"But didn't you realize that she always wore the same outfit?"

"Clearly, you haven't known a lot of kids. They can be stubborn little tics. Heck, when I was in second grade I wore the same pair of shoes for two months."

"I have to admit, I never thought I'd see something like that," Tina said as we all piled into Sinclair's convertible. At least it wasn't red. For a taciturn dead guy, he could be a flashy son of a bitch. "And I've lived a long, long time."

"See what? A ghost? Yeah, it was weird, all right. Man, I'm still creeped out about it."

"Well, try to get a grip on yourself," Sinclair advised, starting the engine, which kicked over with a rumbling purr. "It's inappropriate for the queen of the dead to be afraid of ghosts."

"I must have missed that memo," I grumped.

"I've never seen a ghost before tonight," Tina commented.

"Nor have I," Sinclair added. He backed out of the driveway without looking. Showoff.

"Really? But you guys are so much deader than I am." Hmm, that didn't come out quite right. "I mean, you've been around longer." Way, way, way longer.

"Being able to see and speak with the dead—all dead—is strictly a province of the Queen. And, if she chooses, her Followers."

"Seriously? Huh. How d'you know?"

"Foretold," Tina and Sinclair said simultaneously.

Then Tina added, "It was in the Book of the Dead. 'And the Queene shall noe the dead, all the dead, and neither shall they hide from her nor keep secrets from her.' Like that."

I nearly hit the canvas roof. "Goddamn it. Goddamn it!" Sinclair almost drove off the road and Tina cringed, but I was too mad to care. "I'm *so* sick of this! Something completely weird happens to me, and you guys are all, 'Oh, yeah, that's in the book of the dead, too, did we forget to mention it?'

Well, no more! We're sitting down *right now* and reading the whole nasty thing from beginning to end. Where is it? Is it at the hotel? Let's go find it right now."

"We can't," Sinclair said.

"Why not?"

"Because to read it too long in one sitting is to go insane."

"Oh, that's your excuse for everything," I snapped. I crossed my arms over my chest and wouldn't speak to them until we got to the hotel.

THREE unproductive hours later, I stomped up the sidewalk and through the front door, and immediately threw myself face down on the couch in the entry hall.

"What a fucking disaster," I said to the cushion.

"What's the matter?" It was Marc, standing somewhere to my right. "Are you okay?"

"No."

"They'll come around," Tina said apologetically. "They just need time."

"Ha!"

"What's wrong?" Jessica, hurrying down the stairs. It was amazing how, even though I couldn't see them, I knew exactly where they were. It was amazing that it was almost dawn and they'd been waiting up for me. It was also amazing that this eighty-year-old sofa smelled like popcorn. "Was there another killing?"

"No," Tina said. "We met some other vampires tonight, ones who recently came into town. It . . . ah . . . didn't go well."

"Quite right," Sinclair said, sitting down beside me. "And that's very interesting."

I flopped over and glared at him. Interesting my ass. "How?"

The vampires—there were about half a dozen of them—had done their best to ignore me, and it was so damned chilly in that room from their hostile vibes that I got the shivers.

Oh, they were perfectly deferential to Sinclair, and there was all sorts of "My King" this and "Your Majesty" that, but nobody talked to me at all.

"They're just jealous," Tina said, before Sinclair could answer. She sat down in the chair opposite the couch—this entryway was practically a fourth living room—and looked at me sympathetically. "No vampire in the history of human events has been able to do what you do."

"So?"

"Betsy, you wear a cross around your neck as everyday jewelry! Half the time I can barely look at you."

"Oh, *that* makes me feel better."

"You know what I mean," she said gently. "And in their defense, this has happened very quickly. Many of them have been under Nostro for a hundred years or more. You've been in power for three months."

"So has Sinclair," I pointed out. "And nobody has been giving him the deep freeze."

"Uh," Tina replied, and that was about it.

"They're jerks, but you knew that," Jessica said. "Why's it getting you down now, all of a sudden?"

"Good question. I dunno. It's been a sucky week. And I forgot I was supposed to work tonight. That's twice I had to blow off Macy's. My boss is *not* pleased. And they—the other vamps—they were really cold to me. It was like Antarctica in that hotel room."

"Actually, this is very promising," Sinclair said. "We have our motive."

"What? We do?"

"I was curious to see how out-of-town vampires would react to you, which is why we needed you tonight. And it's patently clear you have aroused much resentment in the vampire community."

"Buncha crybabies."

"I suspect there is a price on your head. In fact . . ." He paused; he had everyone's full attention, and probably found it surprising. "In fact, I suspect these murders are part of a plot to put you out of the way."

"What?" Marc, Jessica, and I all yelped in unison.

Tina was rubbing her eyes. "Oh, shit," she said quietly. "Yes, it fits, doesn't it?"

"Is that why all the other victims were women?" Marc asked skeptically.

Jessica jumped in with, "But why kill other vamps at all?"

"Practice," Tina said. "Working their way up to you, Majesty."

"That's the worst thing I've ever heard!" I sat up in horror. "You guys can't be right. No way!"

"It sort of makes a ton of sense," Jessica said quietly.

"No. That's . . . that's just wrong. On about thirty different levels." Killing people to get in the habit of it? Working their way up to me? I was suddenly swamped with guilt. Poor Jennifer! She wasn't even a true victim; she was *practice*. "Nostro was in power for about a billion years and nobody tried to off him; I'm around since springtime and it's open season?"

"In a word, yes."

"But—"

"You're very threatening to many vampires," Tina said. "You go your own way. You aren't dependent on anyone's protection. You don't need shee . . . ah, human companionship. We have to feed every day, Majesty. *Every* day. As best I can determine, you can go as long as a week without feeding." Actually, my record was ten days, but that was nobody's business. "You are immune to sunlight—"

"If I'm so immune, how come I go down like a rookie boxer whenever the sun comes up?" I grumbled.

"Everyone needs to rest sometime," Sinclair said, managing to sound smug and soothing at the same time.

"Crosses, and holy water," Tina continued to drone. "The Fiends, whom you did not make, obey your every whim. You have a wealthy benefactor.

The king . . ." She trailed off, and it was like she rearranged what she was going to say, because she just finished with, "The king is fond of you also."

Yeah, fond like a wolf is fond of raw beef. "So? Why do they care? It's not like I was overly involved in vampire politics."

"Not yet," Sinclair said.

"Oh. This sucks. This totally and completely sucks. The vampires all hate me and everyone's trying to kill me!"

"Not all," Sinclair said, totally straight-faced. "However, this brings up a vital point: you need a guard. Humans during daytime hours, and loyal vampires in the evening. The Puppet Master isn't likely to stop anytime soon."

This was getting better and better. If I was still alive, I'd have a splitting headache by now. I flopped back down on the couch and sighed. "I just can't believe it." But that was a lie. Tina was right; in a really really bad way, it *did* all fit.

"Keep Sarah close," Tina said after a long silence.

"I concur; she's a good suspect."

"She's a weirdo is what she is, and what are we going to do?" I put my hands over my eyes. "Oh, man, I really need to get out of here." I jumped off the couch and began to pace. "This has been the suckiest week since I died, I swear to God!"

"D'you want to go to Heaven?"

I was touched by the offer, and not a little surprised. Jessica hated shopping, and she practically loathed the Mall of America. I guess when you can buy every single thing six times over, it takes some of the fun out of window shopping.

"No. We can't, anyway . . . it's, like, three o'clock in the morning. The Mall's closed. Even the bars are closed."

"We could go bowling," Marc suggested brightly. "There's a really good twenty-four-hour lane not five minutes from here."

"B-bowling?" The room began to swim. I sat down before I fell—almost in Sinclair's lap. "You mean . . . with . . . with borrowed shoes?"

"What's the *matter* with you?" Jessica snapped at Marc. "Are you trying to make her more upset?"

"Jeez, sorry! I forgot how weird she was about her footwear."

"I'll be all right," I said faintly as Sinclair fanned me with a couch pillow. "I just need a minute."

"The Puppet Master doesn't have to cut off your head," Marc said. "He just has to put you in second-hand shoes. You'll off yourself in despair."

Sinclair laughed, and I snatched the pillow out of his hand and smacked him in the face with it.

Chapter 20

MARIE was waiting for me when I finally went up to my room. I was glad to see her—I'd thought of a couple of things to ask her after we left earlier. And I'd do just about anything, even interrogate the ghost of a kindergartner, to take my mind off the problem *du jour*.

"Still haunting my room, huh?"

"I am not! I just like it in here."

"Uh-huh. Listen, I wanted to ask, how did you . . . uh . . . end up like this?"

She frowned, and a cute vertical line appeared between her eyebrows. "Gee. Nobody's ever asked me that before. O'course, nobody's really talked to me before you came."

Yeah, that whole queen of the dead schtick had all sorts of fringe benefits. I forced a smile as she continued. "Well. My mommy was working here.

We used to sleep in Jessica's room. You know, when Mommy was done working. And once, a bad man came. I heard him come. I woke up and I ran out and saw him hurting Mommy, so I ran over to kick him, and he threw me really hard. And after that, nobody could see me anymore."

She must have hit her head and died, I thought. And then the asshole who tossed her like a tiddlywink buried the body in the front yard. Too bad nobody saw him and called the cops.

And why was that tickling my brain? There was something there, and I just couldn't get to it. Dammit! Why was I great-looking instead of a genius? Usually I didn't mind, but nights like this . . .

"Oh," I said finally, because really, what was there to say? "Well, thanks. I was just wondering."

"I wish my mom would come. I want her real bad."

For sixty years she'd been wanting her! Poor kid. It's funny how that's what was keeping her in the house where she'd been murdered. In the books the spirit can't rest until the killer's been brought to justice, or whatever, but this ghost was just hanging around, waiting for her mom.

In a minute, I was going to start bawling.

"Want to see my new dress?" I asked finally, desperate for a subject change. "I got it on sale. Sixty percent off!"

"Sure."

While I was doing my impromptu fashion show for Marie, I had a brainstorm. *I* would be her mom! I couldn't have kids of my own—I didn't pee anymore, much less ovulate. But I could look after Marie and maybe if she got used to me, she wouldn't miss her mom so much.

This was the most cheerful thought I'd had in a while. The whole "you'll never have a baby—ever" thing had been kind of bumming me out. Not usually, not even every day. But every once in a while that dark thought would sneak back and catch me by surprise.

Not that I wanted to have anyone's babies. Not anyone's in general, and certainly not Sinclair's. Like he could knock me up with his dead sperms, anyway. But still. It would have been nice to at least have the option.

But now I *had* options. I would . . . I would . . . I would adopt ghosts!

Well, okay. Like any plan, it needed work. What the hell, I had time.

THE next night, Jessica and I pulled up outside my father's house. It was much too big for two people, tucked away in the fashionable suburb of Edina, and was too expensive for the housing market. Which made it perfect for my stepmother, Antonia Taylor, aka the Ant.

"Bet they don't have termites," I muttered, staring at the house.

"What?"

"Never mind."

We got out of the car and headed for the front door. Before Jess could knock, I put my arm around her shoulder and said, "I apologize in advance for everything my stepmother's going to say, and everything my father *won't* say."

"That's all right."

"Thanks for coming with me."

"No problem, I'm looking forward to it," she lied. We both knew it was going to be a miserable evening.

It was the traditional Taylor 4th of July BBQ. Due to my father's hectic work schedule—he was the CEO of a company that manufactured sponges—it was taking place on July18th.

The Ant used this party as a chance to show off, so all kinds of people were invited: rich, poor, coworkers, family members, friends, politicians. Jessica got an invitation in her own right because she was rich, which cancelled out the fact that she was black.

"Seriously," I said again, knocking. "I'm very sorry."

"Oh, relax. Think she'll offer me fried chicken and watermelon again?"

I groaned, then forced a smile when my stepmother opened the door.

She blanched when she saw me. This wasn't atypical behavior; I'd have been shocked if she'd smiled. Or even remained expressionless. I'd never been able to forgive her for shattering my parents' marriage, and she'd never been able to forgive me for returning from the dead. It made holidays uneasy, to say the least.

"Happy Fourth of July," I said dutifully.

Ant nodded. "Jessica. Thanks for coming." She left the door open and marched away.

"She thinks your name's Jessica," Jessica stage-whispered.

"Very funny." I followed the Ant into the house. Where, to my total astonishment . . .

"Mom?"

"Hi, sweetie!" My mother put down her drink—Dewar's and soda, from the smell—and threw her arms around me. It was like being embraced by a pillow that smelled like cinnamon and oranges. "I was hoping you were coming." She gave me a hearty smack on the cheek, then grabbed Jessica and gave her the same treatment.

Jess hugged her back, delighted. "Dr. T! What are you doing here?"

A fair question. The Ant despised my mother, and the feeling was heartily mutual. They took great pains not to be in the same town, much less the same room in the same house. I couldn't imagine the bizarre-o set of circumstances that led to my mother's presence in my father's house.

"Don't you remember? I got promoted last month."

"Sure, you're head of the department now." My mom was a professor at the University of Minnesota. Her specialty was the Civil War, specifically the Battle of Antietam. Yawn. "You boss around all those little professor weenies."

"Which rates me," my mother said, smirking, "my own invitation to the Taylor Barbecue Fete."

I rubbed my temples. The Ant's social climbing knew no boundaries. Now she was inviting history professors! This made no sense. Moron. Profs hardly ever got rich. And they could be death at parties. Not *my* mom, of course. But still.

"Thank God," Jessica was saying. "Someone I can talk to who won't mistake me for the help."

"Oh, hush, Jessica, nobody thinks you're the help. Except . . . well, never mind."

"It's swell to see you here," I finally said.

My mom blinked up at me. I'd been taller than her since the seventh grade. "What's wrong?"

"Bad week," Jessica said, snagging a waiter by the elbow and relieving him of a glass of wine. "Undead politics. You know."

"And how's Eric Sinclair?"

"Annoying," I said, grabbing my own waiter. This one was carrying Bloody Marys. I took a gulp and grimaced. I'd like to get my hands on the jerk who decided it was a good idea to wreck tomato juice with vodka and hot sauce. "Arrogant. Obnoxious. Doesn't listen. Shows up uninvited."

"The king of the vampires," my mom murmured. She tried a leer, and failed, instead looking like the Before picture in an antacid commercial. My mom was short, plump, and had white, curly hair. She'd looked like a television grandma when she'd been in her thirties. "And he's quite fond of *you,* sugar-lump."

"Barf," I said, and finished my drink. I scooped a cup of punch off the tray of yet another waiter—how many caterers did the Ant hire, for God's sake? For a "casual barbeque"?

"Err . . . perhaps you should slow down, honey. You're driving, right?"

"Mom, do you know how much booze a vampire needs to drink in order to get tipsy?"

"Well, no."

"Neither do I." A fine night to find out! I finished that drink, too, and downed the rest of Jessica's wine. "Anybody see my dad?"

"He's in the corner with the mayor. Good luck de-ensconcing him. Sweetie, are you really having such a hard time? Do you want me to come and stay with you for a few days?"

I actually shuddered. That's all I needed, my mom running interference while Sinclair and Jon pursued me, the Puppet Master tried to stake me, and the ghost of the dead kid ran around in my room singing "Mary Had a Little Lamb" until I thought I would about go out of my mind.

"Maybe next month, Dr. T," Jessica said quickly, seeing as how I was about to pass out from stress. "It's just . . . complicated right now."

"Never mind, Mom," I said, as nicely as I could. My mother, unlike *some* parental figures I could mention, was totally behind my undead status and tried her best to help me out. She was actually glad I was a vampire; she told me she didn't worry about me being mugged or raped or anything these days. It wasn't her fault my life was so unbelievably—what was Jessica's word?—*complicated*. Yeah, like the wake of a tornado is complicated.

"I think I'm here tonight for another reason," Mom went on, in a lower voice. "Your stepmother appears to be practically bursting with a secret. I suspect The Big Announcement will be tonight."

"Ugh." Oh what, what now? She'd bullied my dad into buying a plane for her shopping trips? She was trying to start another charity ball? "I don't suppose we could leave now?"

"We didn't have to come at all," Jessica pointed out.

I shrugged. In April, when I'd been newly risen, my dad had made it clear he considered me dead, and if I didn't have the good manners to *stay* dead, I should at least stay away. And I'd made it equally clear that I was his daughter, and it was his job to love me, dead or undead. We'd existed in a sort of uneasy truce ever since. I'd been here for Easter dinner a couple months ago, and was here now for the July BBQ. Like it or lump it.

"Have you . . . uh . . . eaten tonight?"

"I'm fine, Mom. Don't worry about it."

"Because I had an idea. Be right back."

She trotted off in the direction of the kitchen, all plump efficiency and speed.

"I cannot believe your stepmother invited your mother to her party."

"I can't believe Mom came!"

Jessica gave me a look. Above the kitchen racket, I heard a blender kick into life. "Of course she came. She wanted to make sure your dad and your Ant were being nice to you."

I smiled for the first time that night. Jess was probably right. My mom looked pleasant, but could be a pit bull if she thought I was in trouble.

Before we could speculate further, Mom returned with what appeared to be a dark chocolate milk-shake.

"It's roast beef," she confided, and I nearly dropped the glass. "I thought, since you can't eat solid foods . . . but you can drink . . ."

"Hmmm," Jessica said, looking at my beef shake.

"Excuse me, ladies, but if you'd take your seats." The waiters were escorting all of us to the big table in the dining room. Interestingly, Ant had seated us at the head of the table, beside her and my dad. Weird! Usually she wanted me as far away from her as possible. Hell, I'd been seated at the kid table until I was twenty-six.

"Hi, Dad," I said, as my father sat down across from me. He flashed me a shaky smile and accidentally knocked over his wine glass.

"Darren," my mother said politely. "You're looking well."

My father smoothed his combover while a waiter righted his glass and blotted the wine stain. "Thanks, Elise. You too. Congratulations again on the promotion."

"Thank you. Doesn't Betsy look charming?"

"Uh, yeah. Charming."

"Thanks, Dad," I said dryly.

"Antonia," Mom said, as the Ant hitched her chair forward in a series of mini-scoots. "Lovely party."

"Thank you, Mrs. Taylor."

Hee! My mom, out of stubbornness and spite, had kept her married name after my dad had ditched her.

"Dr. Taylor," my mom corrected sweetly.

"Jessica," the Ant said. "How are you?"

"Fine, Mrs. Taylor."

"I heard you sold your downtown condo . . . friends of mine almost bought it. Where are you living now?"

"In a mansion on Summit Avenue," she said bluntly, because she knew it would drive my stepmother insane with jealousy. The Ant had been angling for a Summit mansion for years. But, well-to-do as my dad was, that was out of their reach. My mom hid a smile as she went on. "It's much too big for us, of course, but we're managing."

"Oh, err, Betsy's with you?"

"Sure. We're roommates. Along with Marc, our gay pal"—the Ant was a rabid homophobe—"and of course we needed the space because of all the vampires dropping by." And a rabid vampire-phobe.

My mom snorted into her drink. Typical of society parties, nobody noticed what Jessica said, so it wasn't like she'd blown my cover. Besides, even to me, it sounded unbelievable.

I picked up my glass of roast beef and sniffed. Didn't smell too bad. Actually, it smelled kind of good. And the glass was comfortingly warm.

"You tell 'em our news, Toni?" my dad asked, still grimacing over Jessica's announcement.

"News?" my mom asked politely.

"Oh, yes." For the first time all evening, my stepmother looked straight at me. The force of those blue eyes (contacts) and that blond hair (bleached) and those red lips (Botoxed) made me drain my glass of my roast beef in a hurry. Too bad there wasn't some gin in there, too. "Darren and I have exciting news. We're starting a family."

"Starting . . . ?" my mom asked, puzzled.

Jessica's eyes widened. "You mean you're—"

"Pregnant," the Ant said, triumph and hate ringing in her voice. "I'm due in January."

I leaned over and threw up the entire beef shake on my mom's lap.

Chapter 21

"HOW could she?" I moaned. "How *could* she?"

"Because she's jealous of you," Jessica said bluntly. "She has been since the day she moved into your dad's house. She probably thought she was well rid of you back in April. But you were too dumb to stay dead. So, she figures, 'I'll have my own kid, and then I'll get my share of the attention *and* Betsy's.' "

Yep, that was the Ant, all right. To a T.

"I admit," Mom said, "I was surprised. I hadn't expected Antonia to go that route." She laughed suddenly. "Your poor father!"

"He deserves it," I said. I was slumped over in the passenger seat, praying for death. I'd refused to put my seat belt on. Right now, I'd welcome a trip through the windshield. "He picked her. He married her."

"And he's been paying for it ever since, Elizabeth," Mom said in her "don't argue with me" tone. "It's time you grew up and let it go. If *I'm* not angry anymore, why are you?"

"Shut up."

"Beg pardon, young lady?"

"I said, we've showed up. We're here."

My mom gasped as we swung into the driveway. I couldn't blame her. I still half-expected to get thrown out of the mansion myself whenever I ventured past the main hall.

"Oh, Jessica, how marvelous! I suppose it's ridiculously expensive."

"Yeah," she said modestly.

"My goodness! What a palace!"

Jessica, I could see with a sour eye, was lapping this up. I didn't say anything, though I sure felt like it. Jessica's parents died when she was a kid, my mom was the closest thing she'd had to a maternal-type, and Jess adored her.

"Come on up, I've got some sweatpants I can let you have." Mom's skirt was, of course, ruined. Beef shake, bile, and cashmere . . . not a pleasant combo.

"It's really not nec—"

"What, you're going home in your pantyhose? Give me a break. Come on."

"Vampires," Mom whispered to Jessica, "are so touchy."

"I heard that," I snapped.

"Did you really?"

"It sucks," Jessica murmured back. "I can't cut a

fart on the third floor without Bets hearing it on the first."

"Goodness."

As we stepped into the entryway, Marc was walking through carrying a pitcher of iced tea. "Hi, Dr. T. Hey, just in time, you guys! Your guests are here."

"What guests?"

"Um, let's see." Marc started ticking them off on the fingers of his free hand. "There's two of the Blade Warriors, the king of the vampires, the vampire who made *him,* the local parish priest, and one other vampire. Sarah something."

"Great," I griped. "Am I the only one who calls if I'm going to show up at someone's house uninvited?"

"Apparently so," Sinclair said, appearing from nowhere as usual. My mom jumped about a foot. So did I. "Dr. Taylor. A pleasure to see you again."

Mom practically swooned when Eric took her hand in both of his and bowed over them like a dead Maitre d'. "Oh, your Majesty. Nice to see you, too."

"Eric, please, Dr. Taylor. After all, you're not one of my subjects. Pity," he sighed.

"And you must call me Elise," she simpered.

"And I must vomit. Again," I announced. "Will you two stop making googly eyes at each other for five seconds?"

"Forgive my daughter," Mom said, staring raptly up into Sinclair's eyes. "She's normally much more pleasant. She's had a rough night."

"Of course, as she is your daughter, I expect great things of her."

"Why, Eric! How sweet. Betsy never told me you—"

"Seriously, you guys? I'm gonna barf again. So cut it out."

"I will also," Sarah said. I turned; she was standing in the entryway to the second living room. "If we're finished for the evening, I'd like to go."

"No," Sinclair said.

"Yes," I said at exactly the same time. "In fact, why don't *all* of you go? I'm not in the mood."

"Get in the mood. We have serious business to attend to." The frost in his voice melted as he turned puppy eyes to my mother. "Serious vampire business, dear lady, or of course I would insist you join us. We could use a fine mind like yours."

"I want to go!" Sarah shouted. Actually shouted! I thought I was the only one who yelled at Sinclair. "I want to go *now!*"

"What's your problem?" Marc asked. The iced tea pitcher was sweating like Rush Limbaugh in July, and dripping on the floor. He looked around for a piece of furniture less than two hundred years old to set it on, in vain. So he grimly hung onto the pitcher. *Note to self: Buy coasters.* "I heard you don't like this place. What's your damage?"

"If you must know," Sarah said, biting off each word like she'd probably like to bite off Marc's fingers, "I had a daughter once. And she was . . . well, she died. Here. In this house. And I don't want to talk about it and I don't want to be here."

She took a step forward and walked into Sinclair's outstretched arm. I actually heard my jaw muscles creak as my mouth fell open. "You *what?*" I practically screamed.

"A child? A blond girl?" Sinclair asked sharply.

I shouldered him aside. "Is her name Marie? Does she wear headbands to keep her hair out of her eyes? And saddle shoes with anklets? And overalls?"

Sarah burst into tears. This was more shocking than when she yelled at Sinclair. "You know about her? How did you know? Who told you? Don't talk to me about her, I don't want you to do that!"

"Sarah, she's buried in my front yard!"

"She's what?" Jessica asked sharply. "You're forgetting to share again, dead girl."

"Come on!" I pointed up the stairs. "To the vampire bedroom!" I whipped around, which made my mom just about fall over. I must have been moving too fast for her to track again. "Mom, I gotta take care of this right now, okay? We'll talk later, okay? Only this is important. Okay?"

"Of course." She hugged me. "Go do your work."

"Mom." I wriggled free. "You're embarrassing me in front of the other vampires."

I dashed up the stairs.

* * *

I burst into my bedroom, with entirely too many people hot on my heels. "Marie!" I bawled. "Marie, come out!"

She faded into sight. I'd never seen her do it before and let me tell you, it was weird. At first I didn't think she was in the chair, and then the chair looked a little blue around the edges, and then it was like a faded Marie was sitting there, and then a regular Marie was sitting there.

"What?" she asked, looking puzzled. Then she looked past me and her eyes went huge. "Mommy!"

I turned; Sarah would need my help. "Sarah, you can see the ghost if—"

She knocked me into Tina as she lunged past. "Sweetie bug!"

Tina steadied me and muttered, "Sweetie bug?" at the same instant. I felt her pain; it was all I could do not to snicker, too.

Sarah tried to hug Marie, but ended up nearly falling into the chair instead. This did not forestall a lecture. "Mommy, where have you been? I've been waiting and waiting!" Marie had her hands on her hips; she was the picture of outraged patience.

Sarah backed off and tried to answer, but cried harder instead.

"Marie," Sinclair asked, "what did the man who knocked you down look like?"

"Don't ask her about that," Sarah ordered. Her voice was still thick, but her maternal hackles were raised. King or no king, Sinclair wasn't going to cause her kid any pain. I really liked her for it. I felt bad about all the times I blew her off as an icy weirdo. "You don't have to, anyway. It was Nostro. He killed her. And turned me."

"And you were mad at me for killing him?" I asked, aghast.

"It's . . . complicated," she said, my least favorite word of the week.

I heard a *snap* and looked; Tina had picked up the chair and broken one of the legs off of it. "Stop that, the thing's probably worth six figures," I ordered. "Well, now what? I mean, they're reunited." Did this mean Sarah was going to move in, so she could be close to Marie? Shit, I hoped not. If I let one vampire move in, I'd have to let 'em all in!

Sarah was waving her hand through Marie's head.

"Mommy, come *on*. What's taking so long? Let's go!"

Sarah turned toward me. She had aged ten years in ten seconds. Her face was haggard and still she sobbed. "Betsy, my Queen, I need a favor."

"What?"

"Is it—I heard you think we have souls. That vampires have souls."

"Uh . . ." Where was she going with this? I was starting to get a really bad feeling. "Yeah, that's true. I mean, that's what I think."

"So it is true," Sarah said. "Because you're the queen. And your will is our will. So it says in the Book of the Dead."

That thing again. "Okay. I mean, sure, whatever you say."

"Yes. All right."

There was a pause, like she was nerving herself to say something. If she'd been human, she probably would have taken a steadying breath.

"Then I must ask a favor. I'd like you to kill me. Right now."

Chapter 22

"YOU want me to do what?"

"I'll do it," Tina said quickly. I realized that the chair leg she'd been holding would make a good stake. Dammit! Three steps ahead of me, as usual. "The queen shouldn't have to undertake such a low task."

"Uh . . . still having trouble tracking, you guys . . ."

"Low task?" Sarah's eyes were blazing. "My death is not low! It will reunite me with my own flesh and blood, gone from me these fifty years."

"Guys?"

"I only meant . . . the queen doesn't have the stomach for such things," Tina added in a low voice. "But I don't mind, and I'll be glad to help you out."

"Oh." Mollified, Sarah backed off again. "All right, then."

"Sarah, are you sure?" I kept a wary eye on Marie

and practically whispered the rest. "I mean, what if it doesn't work? What if you . . ." *Wake up in Hell,* I'd been about to say, but that probably wouldn't do. "What if I'm wrong?"

"You're the queen," Sarah said, plainly puzzled.

"Besides, you do believe it. In your heart of hearts," Sinclair said. I jumped; he'd been so quiet, I had forgotten he was still in the room. "You know you do. Else why wear the cross? Attend church?"

"How do you know I go to church?"

"Elizabeth, I know *everything* about you."

"Okay, now you've moved from annoying would-be suitor to obsessive stalker. But I'll deal with that later. Give me that thing." Tina slapped the chair leg into my palm like a vampiric O.R. nurse. "Sarah asked me. So I'll do it."

"Thank you, Majesty."

Tina didn't say anything; she just bowed her head.

"Um, *how* do I do it?"

"Aim for the heart," Sinclair said. He touched a spot on Sarah's breast. "Dead center. As quick and deep as you can."

"And that'll . . . do it?"

"Yes. No vampire can recover from a wooden stake through the heart, even if you remove it afterward. She won't disappear like in a silly movie, but she'll be dead for-ever."

I gulped. "Okay. But first, Sarah, you should probably confess. You know, go see God with a clean slate."

Sarah cringed. "Can't I confess to you?"

"No, of course not. Just a second." I snatched open my bedroom door. Ani, Jessica, and Jon nearly fell on me. "Cut it out, you snoops. Father Markus!" I bawled. "Get up here! We need you!"

"I'll get him," Ani said.

"No, *I* will," Jon said, and they were in an instant and furious tussle. Fists flew and they were kicking and scratching like pissed-off chinchillas.

"Uh . . . Jessica . . ."

"Right," she said, stepping over Jon and Ani, locked in combat, and hurrying down the stairs.

"Okay," I said, popping back into my bedroom. "Jess went to get the priest."

"He's not going to touch me with any of his . . . his tools, is he?" she asked, actually trembling. The woman who yelled at Sinclair was scared of an old man in his sixties! "Or sprinkle me with . . . with anything?"

"No. He's just going to hear you out. Just tell him all the bad things you've done—"

"All?" she repeated, appalled.

"Sum up, then," I said, exasperated. "Then I'll stake you through the heart and you and Marie can be together." And then I'll throw up again, and hide under my bed for the rest of the week. A fine plan!

Father Markus could move when he wanted; there was a quick tap at my door and then he poked his head inside. "You called for me?"

"Yeah. Thanks for coming so fast. C'mere,

Father . . ." He shut the door and I quickly gave him the rundown. "So, if you could, you know, make her shiny for God . . ."

"I don't think he can," Tina said. "He can't make the sign of . . . make any signs, or touch her with anything . . ."

"And if she isn't a practicing Catholic, it would be inappropriate, to say the least. Frankly, it's inappropriate anyway, given her . . . ah . . . status." Markus looked around nervously, unfolded his bifocals, and slipped them on. "Are you sure there's a ghost in here?"

"Trust me. Well, just do the best you can." Could a priest do Extreme Unction on a vampire?

Father Markus smiled at Sarah, who was cowering away from him, and I noticed for the first time what a nice face he had. It was long and mournful, like a priestly basset hound, but when he smiled he showed a deeply sunk dimple in each cheek, which was awfully cute.

"Sarah, child." He slowly reached for her hand. She flinched, then let him take it. "Are you heartily sorry for all the sins you've committed, both in life and in death?"

"Yes."

"And do you accept our Lord Jesus Christ as your savior?"

"Eric Sinclair is my Lord," she said, glaring. "And Betsy is my Lady."

"In the afterlife, dear?"

"Well, I suppose so," she grumped. "I mean, if He'll have me."

"Very well, then. I commend your soul to God." He made the sign of the cross over her head and she flinched behind her upraised arm, but nothing happened. She didn't burst into flames or anything like that. I have to admit, I was relieved. I mean, that would have just wrecked the whole evening.

"Thanks, Father," I said.

"Do you need—"

"Bye."

Tina held the door open, pointedly.

"But I'm curious—"

"Vampire business, I beg your pardon," Tina said politely. Then she fixed Ani and Jon with such a withering glare that they instantly lunged for the stairs. Father Markus crept out, throwing one last glance over his shoulder as the door shut.

"Okay." That sounded good; I'd try that again. "Okay. Here we go. Um, Sarah, stand over here." I steadied her against the wall. Then I moved her—my shoes were behind that wall. "Okay, here we go. Um. Okay." I made a practice jabbing motion where Sinclair had pointed. Oh, Lord, how did I get myself into these situations? "Okay."

"Wait!" She grabbed my wrist.

"Oh, thank God."

"No, it's not that. I haven't changed my mind. My clothes. I have a closetful of Armani that I'll never use again. Tina knows where I live. They'll be yours now. You're taller, but we've got the same body type. You can alter most of it."

"Armani?" I flung my arms around her and kissed her chilly cheek. "You won't regret this, I promise."

"Then *get it* done. Please."

"All right, all right."

"Mommy?" Marie, sounding worried.

"Be with you in a minute, baby," Sarah replied, too brightly. Then, hissing, "Do it!"

I did it. I slammed the table leg into her, harder than I had to. I was so afraid I'd wimp out and bungle the job, I overcompensated. The table leg went through Sarah, and through the wall. I let go of it, and Sarah stayed pinned to the wall like a beetle to a card.

And she was gone. I knew she was gone, I could feel it. And if I hadn't been able to feel it, I could sure see it. Her eyes, which had been slitted in rage against my slothful slowness, were glazed over. She was twitching all over like a landed trout, but I knew those for what they were—death spasms.

I turned away, morbidly afraid I was going to barf again. I felt Sinclair's hand on my elbow. "Steady," he murmured. "It was well done. And look!"

I looked. Marie had an expression of intense surprise on her face; she was staring at her hands, which were transparent. She looked up at me and smiled, showing a gap where she'd lost her baby teeth. "I'm going to see Mommy now, B—" Then she popped out of sight.

There was a long silence while the three of us

tried to think of something to say. Finally, Tina spoke up. "I'll dispose of the body."

"Vampires have cemeteries?" I asked shakily. I *felt* shaky, like any second I would fall flat on my face.

She smiled. "Yes."

"Okay. Um, listen. It's been a really long night. An unbelievably long night. Tina, I'm your queen, right? I mean, you've always believed it."

"Of course, Majesty."

"Okay, well, will you do me a really, really big favor? Will you go downstairs and make the Blade Warriors go away, and tell Marc and Jess and my mom I'll see them tomorrow? Because I'm just not up for company right now."

"At once, Majesty." She picked up my hand and—weird and disturbing—kissed it. "You did good." She smiled and her whole face lit up. "You did great."

So how come I felt like a total shit?

I heard Tina tugging and pulling. I refused to look. Then she carried the body out. Sinclair held the door open for her, then closed it behind her. Naturally, he assumed "I don't want company" didn't apply to *him*.

"Well, that's that," I said, staring at the spot where Marie had just been.

"Yes, I suppose so."

"I'm really happy for her."

"As am I."

"I mean, she missed her mom so much, she hung around here for half a century. Years and years! And now they're together. That's good, right?"

"Right."

I burst into tears, and suddenly found myself leaning on something hard and covered with cotton—Sinclair's chest. His arms were around me and he was stroking my back. "Elizabeth, don't cry, sweetheart. Everything you said was right. Everything you *did* was right."

"I know," I wailed into his lapel.

"There, now. You made the hard choice, and that's always difficult." He kissed the top of my head. "But you were a queen to Sarah when she needed you, and Marie couldn't have asked for a truer friend."

He was being so sweet, I cried harder.

"Elizabeth, why do you always smell like strawberries?"

The abrupt topic change startled me in mid-sob. "It's my shampoo."

"Well, it's lovely."

"Also, Jessica threw a strawberry at me earlier. It was the garnish in her daiquiri at my dad's house, and it got stuck in my bra, and I didn't have time to change before you guys came over. I mean, I fished it out, but there was juice and seeds everywhere."

"Well, that's . . . that's lovely, too." I could feel his chest shaking with suppressed laughter.

I jerked back and slapped his shoulder. "It's *not funny,* Sinclair. I'm having a crisis, here."

"Yes, I'm beginning to recognize the signs."

"It's just, I would have looked after her, you know? I had this plan. I mean, I'll never have a baby. So I thought I could sort of take Marie under my wing. And I got used to having her around. She was always around."

"Yes, it must have been unbelievably nerve-wracking."

"No, it . . . I thought, that was okay, right? I mean, once I got over being creeped out by the whole ghost thing. But now I'll . . . I'll never see her again." Just the thought made me cry harder. "That's the only way I'll ever have a kid, is if some other kid gets *murdered* in my house and hangs around!"

"Elizabeth, that's not true."

"It's just been the crappiest week!"

"Yes, it's been difficult for you, hasn't it, poor darling?"

"Yes! And someone's trying to kill me and my house is too big and the other vampires hate me and I'm going to have to crush Jon like a bug one of these days so he quits hanging around and I can see dead people and I think maybe the gardener's a ghost too and my stepmonster's pregnant with my half brother or sister."

He looked at me soberly. "No one will dare to harm you while I'm around." Then, "Who did you say was pregnant?"

"Never mind. You know," I sniffed, "you can be really sweet when you're not driving me up a tree."

"Why, you stole the very words from my mouth," he teased. "Also, I never thanked you for saving my life."

"What? When?"

"When that infant tossed holy water at me. You jumped in front of me and got soaked. Remember?"

"Oh. That. Well, you know." I shrugged. "It was nothing to me. I mean, I knew it wouldn't hurt me. Besides, I wouldn't want anything to happen to that pretty face," I teased.

"Indeed not." He caressed my cheek and I noticed again how very, very black his eyes were. Meeting his gaze was like looking up at the winter sky.

When he leaned in and pressed a kiss to my lower lip, I grabbed his lapels and kissed him right back. He smelled so good—all crisp cotton and his own secret smell. I, of course, smelled like squashed strawberries. Well, he seemed to like it. Also, his tongue was in my mouth and I didn't mind a bit.

"I suppose you'll be ordering me out now," he murmured, breaking the kiss and nipping lightly at my throat, but not breaking the skin. It made me shiver and lean into him.

"Well, I really should. I mean, it's a rotten thing to do."

"What is, darling?"

"I'll just be mean to you again tomorrow. It's rotten to let you stay the night."

He laughed against my neck. He hardly ever laughed, and when he did it was always startling and kind of fun, like finding a ripe orange in your mailbox. "I'll risk it," he said, and shrugged out of his jacket.

I stood back and watched him disrobe. It was amazing how quickly the clothes were flying off him. God, he had a great body. A farmer's son, Sinclair had been in excellent shape when he died. His shoulders were so broad he had to have his suits tailor-made, and his arms were tautly defined with muscle. His chest was lightly furred with black hair, tapering to a narrow waist and long, muscular legs. And he was very happy to see me.

"This doesn't mean anything, does it?" I asked, although it was suddenly hard to talk . . . my tongue felt too thick for my mouth. "There's not another little passage in the Book of the Dead that maybe you forgot to mention? If we have sex again does this make you, like, super king forever and ever?"

"No." He turned me around and unzipped my dress. He nuzzled the back of my neck. "You're . . . ah . . . not planning on talking the entire time, are you?"

I whipped back around. My dress fell to my feet in a silk puddle and I saw his eyes widen appreciatively—for a change, I was wearing matching underwear. Pale green, with monarch butterflies. "What's *that* supposed to mean?"

"Oh, nothing. Chat away, dear. I'll be all ears." He laughed again and hugged me to him. This was quite interesting, as I could feel his hard length pressing against my lower stomach, so I decided to forget about being annoyed. "Oh, Elizabeth. I'm really, really quite fond of you."

"Yeah, I can tell. Well, I like you, too, Eric, when you're not being a shit."

"In other words, when I'm buckling under. A

fine platform on which to base a thousand year relationship."

For once, that thought wasn't completely terrifying. And he was so strangely cheerful, it was perking me right up. Frankly, I'd never seen him in a better mood. The man must absolutely love getting laid. "Let's just take it one day at a time, all right?"

"As my queen commands," he said, and scooped me up, and tossed me on the bed. "Also, I like your butterflies. But I think they should be on the floor, don't you?"

And in a moment, they were.

"WOW."

"Yes."

"I'm panting. I'm actually out of breath, and I don't need to breathe. Day-amn!"

Sinclair stretched, then pulled me to his side and pressed a quick kiss to my breast. "Art comes in many forms."

"Oh, so you're an artist, now?"

"Yes."

I snorted, but didn't disagree. He'd been hungry, and skillful, and very, very good. Of course, he had about sixty years of experience. My throat still stung where he'd bitten me, but I wasn't holding it against him. I knew he'd been completely unable to help himself.

I wondered if he hurt where I'd bitten him.

I laid there next to him and tried to think about

how to tell him my dirty little secret. Because it had happened again. When we were making love, I could read his mind. But I knew he couldn't read mine. I'd tried to send thoughts to him before, but with absolutely no reaction. And I wasn't smart enough to figure out a tactful, nonthreatening way to share this with him.

Say, Sinclair, did you know that when we're having sex, I can read your every thought and desire? This isn't going to bother someone as tightly controlled as you, is it?

Pass.

"Say, are you sure you want to spend the night? What if the Puppet Master makes another go at me?"

"Let him try," Sinclair said, pulling the comforter over us. "I've been fantasizing about pulling his head off for the last few days."

"You know, *most* people fantasize about getting married, or building a dream home, or going on vacation somewhere nice."

"I think about those things, too," he said seriously.

"Oh, is this the part where we share intimate small talk and fall in love?" I teased.

I could feel him studying me in the dark. "No," he said finally. "Go to sleep."

Sure! It'd be so easy, because it wasn't like I had a ton of stuff on my mind or anything. Shoot, I was still replaying the really excellent sex I'd just had. *Really* excellent.

I could still feel his hands on me. Actually, his

hands *were* on me. But earlier, they'd been everywhere. And he'd kissed me everywhere, too. He'd been like a starving man in an Old Country Buffet restaurant.

And I mean *everywhere*. Sinclair had practically taken up residence between my legs. When his tongue had snaked inside me, I'd just about gone out of my mind. He licked and kissed and sucked, and I was so busy begging him not to stop that at first I thought he'd been talking out loud.

"Don't bite her, don't bite, don't bite, don't bite . . ."

"What's the matter?" I'd gasped.

"Nothing. Hush," he'd said, and flicked my clit with his tongue.

". . . bite don't bite don't bite don't bite don't don't don't . . ."

I grabbed his shoulders and tugged until his chest was settling against mine. "That's nice," I had managed. "Are you going to fuck me now?"

I expected a sarcastic response or one of those annoying "as my queen commands" sneers, but instead he shoved my legs further apart with his knee and surged inside me. I could practically feel him in the back of my throat; he was really hung, and that was just fine.

". . . bite don't bite don't bite don't bite don't you'll scare her don't bite don't . . ."

I wrapped my legs around his waist, urging him closer as he stroked, and pressed his face into the side of my neck. The muscles in his shoulders were rigid with strain; they felt like rock beneath my fingers.

Then I bit him. He stiffened in my embrace and shuddered all over; his cool, rich blood flooded my mouth and the sensation of taking from him while he took from me tipped me over into orgasm.

I barely felt his teeth break my skin; I was shuddering around him and realized that high whimpering sound was coming from me.

We were rocking together so fiercely my giant, heavy bed was actually moving; the headboard was slapping the wall and I imagined the house was probably shaking, too. At least, it should have been. It felt like the universe should be affected by what we were doing; it wasn't just a couple of lonely people having sex. For the first time, I had a real sense of who we were, and what we were about. The king and queen of the dead were making love so fiercely, chunks were falling out of the wall.

Elizabeth!

"Eric," I'd managed.

He thrust once more, harder than he had before, the headboard gave a final slam, I came again, and so did he. His grip tightened until it was just short of painful, and then he was licking the bite mark on my neck, and I was gasping and out of breath.

"Jesus!"

"I've asked you before not to call me that," he said, and we both cracked up.

Yeah, it had really been something. The question was, could I now read anyone's mind during love-making, or just Eric's? And how much longer should I keep this to myself?

I heard a *crack* and flinched; Sinclair had snapped his fingers in front of my face. "Are you in there? I've been saying your name for the last ten seconds."

"Sorry. I was thinking. And don't do that; you know I hate it."

"Thinking about?"

"Actually, about how amazing you are in bed." Well, it was mostly the truth. "I hate to tell you anything that'll make your head bigger than it already is, but yum!"

"Thank you," he said politely, but he sounded pleased. "Of course, you bring out the best in me. Your body is a feast."

"Well, I'm trying to slim down. Seriously, you're the best I've ever had."

"Oh? Out of, say, how many?"

"Forget it, pal. We're not doing this."

He yawned and cuddled me into his side. "Why not?"

"Because you'll win. You've been having sex a lot longer than me."

"True. But I'm curious about the others you've invited into your bed."

"Let's just say I could count them on one hand and leave it at that." Actually, three fingers. But that was none of his business.

"Practically a virgin," he mused.

"Oh, hush up. Hey, is it getting lighter in here or is it just *mmmmmm* . . ."

The last thing I remember was Eric chuckling as I sank into unconsciousness. Stupid sunrises!

Chapter 23

I opened my eyes and was not at all pleased to see Marc standing over me. His mouth was hanging open and he was gaping down at me. And presumably, Sinclair, who had at one point kicked off the covers.

"What?" I leaned over Sinclair, grabbed the comforter, and spread it over us. "Somebody better be on fire, pal."

"Huh? Oh. Uh . . . sorry, the reason I came up here has been driven completely out of my head by the sight of your cellulite."

"I don't have any," I snapped.

"Neither do I," Sinclair said. "Good evening, by the way."

Jessica walked in. She slowed as she saw Sinclair next to me, then pretended like she hadn't just had the crap shocked out of her and strode briskly over to Marc. "Are you going to give her the phone or what? It's your boss," she added to me. "He sounds pissed."

I grabbed for the phone, which wasn't easy because Marc was still staring, and I had to wrestle it away from him while remaining modestly covered.

"Hello? Mr. Mason?"

"Elizabeth. You were supposed to be here an hour ago."

Shit! What day was it? What *time* was it? Wait a minute . . . "Mr. Mason, I switched with Renee for tonight. She's covering my shift."

"Oh? Because Renee isn't here, either."

Well, hell, go yell at *her*. "Mr. Mason, I'm not on tonight."

"The schedule disagrees."

"Yeah, but . . . we switched!"

"I see. Do you think you could come in for a couple of hours, since Renee seems to have forgotten your . . . ah . . . arrangement?"

"Sure," I said quickly. I was going to have to do some serious damage control on this one. "Be there in an hour."

"Good-bye, Elizabeth."

"Shit!" I said as he hung up. "He thinks I'm lying to cover my ass."

"And what an ass," Sinclair said admiringly.

"You stop that. Dammit, now I've got to go in and be all nicey-nice and kick Renee's butt up to her shoulderblades when I see her."

"At the same time?"

"Dammit!"

"Mason takes you for granted," Jessica declared.

"You're sweet, but I haven't been a very good employee lately, what with my—"

"Secret vampire life?"

"Well . . . yeah."

"Slut," Marc coughed into his fist.

"I am not! I've only had sex twice in the past . . . what year is this?"

Sinclair laughed.

"You guys go away," I ordered. "I have to grab a shower and get ready for work."

"The Blade Warriors are here," Jessica said, rolling her eyes. "Well, one of them."

I rubbed my temples. "It's Jon, isn't it?"

"If Jon's the one who looks like he should be on a beach with Gidget and her pals, yes."

Sinclair growled. Actually growled, like a wolf or something! "Send him away," he ordered.

"Calm down, O king of the dead people," Jessica said, smirking. "As it happens, he's insisting on talking to Bets, here."

"I could not care less. Send him away."

"Stop ordering my friends around!" I rested my chin on my fist. "Nuts. Well, I can't talk to him right now, I've got to get to work. I'll have to see him later. Nobody's died, though, right?"

"Not yet."

"Cheerful thought," I muttered, standing. What did I care? Jessica'd seen me naked about a million times, and Marc was a lot more interested in how

Sinclair looked. "All right. I'll catch you guys later."

"Oh, come on," Marc whined. "We want to hear about what happened up here last night. Specifically, why Tina came down the stairs carrying a dead vampire. And why you didn't wake up by yourself."

"Later," I said firmly, and walked into the bathroom.

I was rinsing shampoo out of my hair when I heard someone pull back the shower curtain. "You'd better be anyone but Eric Sinclair," I said without opening my eyes.

"You'd prefer Marc? Or perhaps Jon?"

"Ugh, and again . . . ugh." I finished rinsing and opened my eyes. Eric was splendidly nude (still!), standing in front of me with his hands on his hips, smiling. "He's just a kid with a crush."

"You sound unsurprised."

"For some weird reason," I admitted, "teenage boys really like me."

"I can't think why," he said, idly tweaking my nipple.

I slapped his hand away. "What's got you in such a good mood? That's the second smile this morning. Evening, I mean."

"Oh, I guess I'm just an evening person." He grabbed me to him and rubbed his chest across mine. "More of that strawberry shampoo, I see."

I tried to wriggle away, but I was too slippery. I was like a trout in a live well. Nowhere to go! "Cut that out. I don't have time for your shenanigans. I'm late already." But hoo, man, was I tempted! No. I couldn't. My job in Heaven depended on *not* getting sweaty with Eric right now. Dammit! "Did I say I'm late? Because I really am."

"Spoilsport," he said, but he released me. "Why you insist on dashing off to a meaningless—"

"Don't start."

"I wasn't," he said, having the gall to sound wounded.

I tossed him the soap, which he snatched, one-handed, out of the air. "Sure you weren't. Lather up, big boy, and then it's time to hit the bricks."

"You can make getting clean sound so . . . dirty."

I laughed in spite of myself. "Don't start, I said!"

"I hear and obey," he replied, and then squeezed my shampoo bottle—*when* had he grabbed that? Strawberry gel arched out and splattered across my breasts.

I cursed, and ducked under the spray again to rinse. Then we ran out of hot water—stupid ancient water heater!—and we were both cursing.

I was headed down the back stairs—the quickest way from my room to the driveway behind the kitchen—when I heard Jon's plaintive, "But she *likes* me. I can tell!" and froze in mid-step.

I started to creep back up. I'd take the other stairs, go around the front way, but Jessica's words glued me to the spot.

"Jon, she's not just a vampire. Although that would be problematic enough, don't you agree? You and your little group of nerd hoods kill vampires."

"Only the bad ones," he said. "We voted. Sinclair and Tina and Betsy and Monique are off-limits. We were still trying to figure out about Sarah when she . . . well, whatever you guys did to her. But if we catch a vampire trying to hurt or kill a human, he's fair game."

"Spare me your twisted machinations. And you might want to run that plan by Sinclair."

"He's not my boss!"

"Okay, okay, don't burst a blood vessel. My point is, Betsy's not just *a* vampire, she's the *queen* of the vampires."

"So? She doesn't even like that job. And the way I hear it, it's an accident that she's even queen, anyway. She'd get out of it if—"

"Yeah, but she can't."

"If she really wanted to—"

"No, really, she can't. I guess the vampires have this book with all their laws and prophecies and stuff in it, and according to that book—which is like the vampires' bible, so they pay attention to it—Betsy's the queen and Eric Sinclair is the king."

"So?" Sulky now, not that I could blame him. It's not like Jess was telling him anything he wanted to hear.

I heard her shift her weight and almost grinned. She was losing her patience, and trying her best not to lose her temper as well. "So, it's like they're married. In the eyes of vampire law, they *are* married. Not only are you lusting after a vampire, you're lusting after a married one."

"So?"

"Don't be such a moron. They've got a kingdom to run, Jon, and in case you haven't noticed, the king is crazy about her. He'll pull your head off if you try anything. And be fair, it's not like Betsy's encouraged you. Right?"

Sullen silence.

"Besides . . . I think . . . maybe . . . she loves him, too."

"No."

I nearly fell down the stairs. Damn right, no!

"Oh, it's the best kept secret in the world. Even from her! But I guess my point is, why don't you drop this whole thing? She'll just keep rejecting you. Or, Eric will pull your head off. So we're looking at a lose/lose situation, right?"

"I'm still asking her out."

I heard a whoosh as Jessica threw her arms in the air. "Fine, get your head handed to you, see if I care."

"If she says no, she says no. But I'm asking anyway."

Great. Well, I'd field that one when I came to it. As for right now, the front stairs awaited. And so did Macy's!

I actually laughed while pulling out of the driveway; I couldn't help it. The idea was too absurd. Me, in love with Eric Sinclair? And *him* in love with *me?* Even sillier.

I drove him nuts. I knew it. He knew it. We all knew it. The only reason he even liked having me around was because I was the queen. Beyond that, we had nothing in common. Ab-so-lu-te-ly nothing. It was silly enough that we were destined to rule at each other's sides for, like, a zillion years. He had to be as annoyed about that as I was.

My cell phone buzzed. *Boop-boop-boo-BOOP-BOOP-boop bip boop boop!* Stupid "Funkytown" theme; I've got to get that changed. I fished it out of my purse. "Hello?"

"As usual," Jessica announced, "you've left an enormous mess for me to clean up."

"Sorry about that, but I had to get to work."

"And *what* did you do to Sinclair? He's humming! And he did the dishes! 'High time to earn my keep,' he says, and then he mojo'd the housekeeper into taking a nap. You should see the guy in Playtex rubber gloves."

I cracked up. "You're making that up."

"Who could make something like that up? And he shows no desire to leave, either—usually he does a fade when he finds out you've left. Not tonight. I keep tripping over the guy. It's creepy, but interesting."

"Yeah? Who's all there?"

"Everybody. Jon, Ani, Father Markus, Tina. Oh, I almost forgot the best part! After doing the dishes and rearranging your bookcase—all the titles are facing the right way, now—"

"Goddamn it!"

"He runs into Jon, who has got it *bad* for you, FYI—"

"I heard."

"Anyway, I figured they'd sort of growl at each other and beat their chests like gorillas on the Nature channel, but Sinclair just smiled at him and patted him on the head. Patted him on the head! Good thing I hid Jon's crossbow in the fridge or there'd have been real trouble."

"That *is* weird," I admitted.

"Weird, shit. It's bizarre and unprecedented, is what it is. You must have knocked his brains loose."

"Jessica!" Then I snickered. "Okay, well . . . maybe I did."

"What, did you grow an extra breast or something? And don't think I didn't notice the big chunks that fell off the ceiling in your room. I'm telling you, I've never seen this guy in such a good mood."

I swerved to avoid a red BMW—I hate those 'I've got a yellow light so I have the right of way' drivers. "Look, we had a nice night, okay? A very nice night. I was upset about the Ant, you know, and having to stake Sarah—"

"*You* killed her?"

"—and all the stuff that's been going on lately, and he, you know. He made me feel better."

I could feel Jessica leering through the phone. "I bet."

"Oh, stop it."

"Well, watch out for Jon-boy. He's determined to ask you to the sock-hop, or whatever kids his age do for fun."

"Sock hop? Cripes."

"Should have stayed dead," Jessica advised, "like a normal person."

"Oh, shut up."

"Spray it, don't say it," she said, then hung up on me so she could get the last word. Jerk.

Chapter 24

"I'M *fired?*"

"We're going to have to let you go," Mr. Mason explained. "When you're here, Elizabeth, you do fine work, but of late you've become unreliable."

"But . . . but . . ." But I can't help it. But I'm the queen of the undead, and queens didn't get fired! But I've been really busy trying not to get murdered! But the new Pradas are coming in next week and I desperately need my employee discount! But I've never been fired by someone wearing a turtleneck in July! "But . . . but . . ."

"Besides, don't you have more pressing business to attend to?" he added kindly. "You've got a killer to catch, and a consort to satisfy."

"Yeah, that's true, but—*what?*"

"You shouldn't be here, Majesty. Everyone appears to grasp this but you."

I gaped at him. Started to speak, couldn't, gaped some more. Tried to talk again. No luck. I had been struck mute with shock, just like when Charlize Theron won the Oscar for Best Actress.

He opened the lone manila folder on his otherwise spotless desk, and withdrew a paycheck, which had a blue piece of paper stapled to it. Termination form. Argh! "Here's your final check. And good luck catching the killer."

"Mr. Mason!"

"Oh, I'm not a vampire," he said, correctly reading my bulging eyes and sprung jaw. "I'm Kept."

"You're what?"

"I'm a sheep," he clarified. He tugged at his cashmere turtleneck, baring his throat. There wasn't a bite, but there was a pretty good bruise. "At first, when you came here, I thought it was a test. Or a joke. Then, I realized you were serious. You really wanted to work here. I couldn't think why. Finally, I realized I must fire you for your own good."

"Thanks tons," I said, starting to recover from the shock. "Jeez, why didn't you tell me sooner?"

He coughed into his fist. "I assumed you were smart . . . er . . . I thought you knew what I was."

I snatched my check and stood. "Well, you were wrong about me, mister! So there!" Wait a minute. Oh, never mind. "This is just perfect. The perfect end to a perfect week."

He spread his hands apologetically. "I do apologize. And I wouldn't advise trying to snare me to get me to re-hire you. After all this time, I'm immune to everyone but my master."

"But . . . but if you know me, you must have recognized Eric Sinclair. And he zapped you pretty good."

"His Majesty the King," Mason said carefully, "is a very powerful vampire. You're quite right; I could not resist falling in thrall."

"Thrall? Falling in thrall? I don't know what the hell you're talking about, but I'm leaving before I pull your head off your shoulders and use it for a soccer ball."

"And I appreciate it. It really is for your own good, you know," he called after me as I stomped out. I made a rude gesture queens probably weren't prone to. Felt pretty good, though.

I trudged out to my car, which was parked in Georgia. Stupid gigantic Mall of America parking lot. What a rotten week. I couldn't imagine it getting any worse. Well, I suppose I could get decapitated. That might be worse. On the other hand, my troubles would pretty much be over.

I rested my forehead on my car roof. The body shop had done a good job of patching up the bullet holes and arrow gouges. And it ran like a dream. Too bad I just didn't have the energy to fish out my keys and get in. I'd probably run over a little kid on the way home, or have to break up another vamp/human unfair fight. Something. Something bad, guaranteed.

I heard a car pull up behind me, but didn't turn. What fresh hell was this? Probably the Ant, loaded down with crucifixes and baby formula.

"Majesty?"

I turned; it was Monique. She had opened her car door, a sleek black Porche, and was half-in, half-out of it. She looked gratifyingly concerned, which cheered me up a little. "What's wrong, my Queen?"

"Everything!"

She blinked at me.

I started banging my head against the roof. It didn't hurt a bit. "Every single thing in the whole world, *that's* what's wrong."

"Majesty, you're denting your car roof," she observed.

"Oh, who cares? I'd elaborate on my grotesque and numerous problems, but then I'll probably start to cry, and it'll be really awkward."

"I'm willing to take a chance. Why don't you leave your car and come with me? We can get a drink and you can tell me who you want me to kill."

"Don't tease me," I sighed. "And that's the best offer I've had all day. Okay."

I abandoned my car without a thought and practically jumped into Monique's Porsche. "Let's book."

Chapter 25

"THAT does sound bad," Monique admitted when I finally wound down. She downshifted to make the yellow light, which showed off what pretty legs she had. Black miniskirt, black heels, white blouse with lace cuffs. Tarty, but trendy. "But at least the king is firmly in your corner."

"Ha! Firmly in my pants is more like it."

"Ah-*hum*. So . . . how is he?"

"Annoying."

"I mean . . . are his sheet skills adequate?"

"I have to admit," I admitted, "I've never heard it put quite like that. And yeah. They're more than adequate. I mean, he's really fine. Whoo! I could sweat just thinking about it. If I still sweat."

"Do tell!"

To a near stranger? Even a nice one? No thanks. "But it doesn't mean anything to him. He just likes sex. You should have seen what he was doing the first time I went to his house!"

"He seems," Monique said carefully, "to be an acceptable consort."

"Sure, if you don't mind being bossed around. And condescended to. And hugged when you're upset. And made love to until your toes curl. And-uh-look, let's talk about something else."

"As you wish." She wrenched the wheel as we turned onto Seventh Avenue—practically on two wheels, yikes!—and pulled up outside a small brownstone with a screech. I thought it was an apartment house, but the doors were propped open and there was a line of extremely hip-looking people stretching down the sidewalk. The red neon sign over the doors read SCRATCH.

"Oh, dancing?" I asked, brightening. "I love to dance."

"This is my club. I've been longing to show it to you."

"Oh, yeah?" Well, that explained the nice clothes. And the Porsche. "I didn't think you were from around here."

"I have properties all over the country. It's amazing what you can do when you've got seventy years to get it done."

"Good point," I said, as a valet held the door open. He was wearing black cargo pants, tennis shoes with no socks, and a white t-shirt with green lettering: GO FANG YOURSELF. Very cute. He smirked at me as he slammed the door shut and another valet drove Monique's car away. "So, this is like a vampire club?"

"Mostly. Come along, Majesty, let's get you a drink."

"Sounds good to me." We brushed past the waiting crowd and I followed her like a sheep to slaughter. Hmm. I *was* following her, and I certainly didn't mind, but why did that corny saying creep me out all of a sudden?

And why, now that Monique and I had entered the club, had everyone stopped dancing? And why were they all staring at us?

"You know," Monique said, turning to me, "you really don't deserve him."

"Who?" I asked dumbly. Sheep to slaughter? Where had I heard that before? Mr. Mason, of course. He said he was Kept. A sheep. And where had I heard that icky term before Mason? From Monique, the night Tina and she were attacked. She said it was much easier when you kept sheep, instead of hunting all the time. And Tina and Sinclair had blown it off, hadn't wanted to explain. Too late now. Too bad for me. "Who don't I deserve?" Except I had a horrid feeling I knew exactly who she was talking about.

"The king, of course."

"Yeah, of course. Uh . . . you didn't put Mr. Mason up to firing me or anything, did you?"

She just looked at me.

"Yeah. 'Course you did. He lied about Renee not coming in, so he could fire me and get me out of the building. And then . . . uh . . . he tipped you off, I guess, so you knew where I'd be, and now we're here. In your place."

"I knew you were foolish," she sighed as several hands grabbed me from behind, "but I didn't think you were a moron."

"What's the difference?" I yelled as I was dragged to the middle of the dance floor. Unfortunately, I didn't think it was because they wanted to do the Lambada with me. "And who's a moron? I figured it out, didn't I? Hey! Cut it out! Hands to yourselves, creeps. Monique, what the hell . . .?"

Monique disappeared behind the bar, and reappeared with a wicked-looking stake as long as my forearm.

"And here I thought you were mixing me a daiquiri."

"This is your cue," she said, as if explaining to a slightly retarded student, which I resented the hell out of, "to say something obvious, like, 'you're the killer.' "

"Well, you are! I can't believe it! The *one* new vampire I meet who's actually nice, and you're going around killing vampires!" There were still about ten hands on me and they held me firmly. Where was Sinclair when I actually wanted him around?

"Yes," she said, sounding bored. Gosh, it was too bad I wasn't able to capture her full attention. I was getting so mad, I felt like biting myself. "I had this insane idea that you might be difficult to bring down. So I wanted the Warriors to get some practice.

Then . . . *then,*" she added, and her lip curled, and she looked truly furious for the first time, "that idiot, that infant, that moron, Jon, fell under your spell. And he wouldn't kill you for me anymore. And he persuaded the others to stop, too."

I shrugged modestly. It wasn't my fault I had unholy sex appeal. "Too bad, you cow. And will you guys get *off?*" I yanked and pulled, to no avail. Were they rubber vampires, or what? "*And* you set yourself up to be attacked, to throw suspicion away from yourself."

She yawned. "Mmm-hmm."

And it worked, too, dammit. I'd never considered Monique for a second. I was too busy keeping a wary eye on Sarah, who was worth about twenty of this treacherous bitch. To think I staked *her* and decided to go party with Monique. God, I was really too stupid to live sometimes. However, it didn't look like that was going to be a problem much longer.

"Well, now you're gonna get it. I guess. Yeah! Big trouble, Monique." As soon as I freed myself from the grip of the RubberMaid Undead. "Any second now, and I'll . . . uh . . ."

"So, I'll kill you," she finished, perking up, "and Sinclair will be in need of a new consort, and of course Tina won't do. They're more like siblings, have you noticed? And Sarah's dead, and there aren't many of us who are suitable, you know."

"So that leaves you, huh?"

"That leaves me."

"But aren't there thousands of us?"

"I can assure you, Eric Sinclair will find me the most viable choice."

"And the fact that he has a consort right now," I said dryly, "isn't an impediment, or anything."

"Impediment! I'm amazed you didn't need a flashcard to use the word."

"Hey, hey! Assaulting me is one thing, but watch the nasty comments."

She stalked toward me, stake in hand. I became morbidly aware that we had an audience. Besides the vampires hanging onto me with grim determination, there were about twenty more on the dance floor who were staring at us. No help, I figured. They belonged to Monique. Or they didn't think I was a real queen. Either way, it amounted to the same thing. Well, at least she was still talking, even if she was waving that stake around like a band leader's baton. Classic James Bond villain mistake. I hoped.

"Waste of resources."

"What? I wasn't listening."

She gritted her teeth. "I said, I am appalled at the waste of vampires and resources. I should have taken you myself, the moment I came to town. I had no idea you'd be so easy."

"Hey! What'd I say about the nasty stuff?"

"To think I was paying the Blade Warriors to practice, to hone their skills, to work their way *up* to you. What nonsense! You didn't really kill Nostro, did you?"

"What?" The abrupt subject change took me by

surprise. "Is that why you thought I'd be such a toughie?"

She gave me a withering "of course" look.

"As a matter of fact, I *did* kill him, so there." Alas, like little George Washington, I could not tell a lie. "Well, sort of. I set the Fiends on him, and they ate him." The Fiends! What I wouldn't give to see their snarling faces right now. "But listen, Monique. You don't have to stake me to get Sinclair. You can *have* him."

"I disagree."

"No, really!" I couldn't believe this. First he tricked me into boinking him. Then I found out I was his undead little woman for a thousand years. Then he tricked me into boinking him again. Well, sort of. Now this nutty bitch was going to kill me to have him for herself! Oooh, if I lived through this, he was getting a piece of my mind.

A pox on you, Eric Sinclair!

"Seriously. I don't want him, I never wanted him." Okay, that last one was a small lie. I mean, I *wanted* wanted him, you know, like you want a juicy steak, but I didn't want to be married to him, not without him at least asking. Which he never did. Not once. Was that so much to ask? A marriage proposal? I didn't think so. Not that anybody asked my opinion. Oh, God forbid, anybody should ask my opinion!

". . . is devoted to you."

"What?"

"Will you pay attention? In case you haven't noticed, you're in dire straits."

"Yeah, yeah. I've been there before. Look, we can work this out. Sure, you're a crazy cow bent on my destruction, but can't we get along? I mean, if my parents could work things out, anybody can. You can have Sinclair on Mondays, Wednesdays, and Fridays, and I—"

She lunged forward with a scream of frustration—I'll admit I have that effect on people—and buried the stake in my chest. It hurt like a son of a bitch. And then I died. Again.

Chapter 26

FROM *the private papers of Father Markus, Parish Priest, St. Pious Church, 129 E. 7th Street, Minneapolis, Minnesota.*

Moments too late! I suspect that's why we were all so slow to react. It didn't seem real that we hadn't arrived in time to save the day. The children, especially, had no real experience in failure. The cavalry always arrives in time, at least in the movies.

Jon had followed Betsy all over town, of course—foolish boy, we had all warned him it was hopeless—and something about the club put him on alert. Possibly the way all the vampires waiting outside ran off for no apparent reason. They must have sensed something in the air—shifting allegiences, perhaps. It didn't matter now.

The important thing was, Jon called us when he

got to Scratch. It didn't take long for us to arrive, in terms of mileage. In terms of time, of course, it took just a few moments too long.

When the woman who had been pulling our strings killed Betsy, it was like all the light went out of the room. Exactly like that. We were so shocked, nobody moved.

And Betsy was still, so still. It seemed ridiculous that those green eyes would never again flash fire, that her red lips would never form the words *idiot* or *moron* or *asshole* ever again.

Then Eric Sinclair, as formidable and frightening a creature as I have met in my long days, just went to pieces. It would have been touching if it hadn't been so terribly, terribly sad.

He cradled her in his arms and sank to the floor. His coat billowed around them as they fell. He whispered her name, over and over, and caressed her face with trembling fingers, and blocked all of us out.

Our former employer, Monique, tried to explain herself. She could smell death in the air—her own, as well as the Queen's. We were all standing in silent judgement, but she must have known it wouldn't last. That we would soon be moved to action. She had been caught out, her true colors revealed at the worst possible moment, and she knew it as well as we did.

It was the usual, tedious motive: she explained that she had coveted Eric, who by vampire law belonged to Betsy. So Monique had formed the Blade Warriors to get Betsy out of the way.

Was she crazy, I wondered disapassionately, or just driven? Had years of feasting on humans warped her conscience until hiring children to kill her own kind actually seemed like a fine plan? I didn't know. And at the moment, frankly, I didn't care.

But she might as well have been speaking to a boulder. Despite her pleadings for his attention, Eric Sinclair simply rocked Betsy in his arms and wouldn't look up or speak.

Tina, however, had no such compunctions. She was as angered and shocked as any of us, but she was not frozen to inaction. I have long been fascinated by how different vampires are on the outside from their true selves. Tina had always looked like a charming sorority girl to me.

Not tonight.

She led the charge, and in minutes, a vicious fight was raging all around us. I pulled Marc and Jessica behind me—they were too stunned to fight—and held out my cross, but I needn't have bothered. I could see several of Monique's minions were slipping out the back, avoiding the fight entirely. Wise of them. Because when Mr. Sinclair recovered his wits, this would not be a good day to be on Monique's side.

Being human, I of course could not track much of the fight. It was a physical impossibility. There would be a flash of silver or a blurred fist, and then a vampire's head would be rolling on the floor, or a body would sail through the air. And the children, as always, acquitted themselves well.

Finally, only Monique was left, and Jon, who had tears in his eyes, pulled his knife and marched toward her. He ignored us, he ignored everything. He swung it back, and I heard him say, "This is for Betsy, you bitch," only to be stopped in mid-swing by Tina's sharp, "Hold!"

For she had moved with that eerie, inhuman quickness, and was now holding our common enemy at swordpoint—Ani's sword, in fact—and had an arm out to prevent Jon from getting closer.

Monique had been backed into a corner, and Tina, despite her fragile looks, was formidable. Ani was backing her up, but it appeared to be entirely unnecessary.

"We'll let the king decide her fate," Tina said, and that was that. Even Jon, heartbroken, could not argue with that command.

I noted much of the heart had gone out of Monique's group when Eric Sinclair arrived. It made sense, though it was unfair and unkind to dear Betsy. Because if she hadn't seemed especially royal or noble—although she was, if one cared to take the trouble to really *see* her—there was never any question of Eric's right to the throne. And nobody wanted to mess with the most powerful vampire on the planet. Especially when he had just lost his consort to treachery and betrayal.

The last of Monique's vamps slipped out, and we let them go. We had been woefully outnumbered, and weren't unaware of the depths of our luck.

While Tina held Monique at bay, the rest of us crouched around Betsy. There was no blood and, as I wrote earlier, the whole thing didn't seem quite real. She did not look like a dead woman. The stories were wrong. The movies were wrong. She wasn't a pile of dust, she wasn't a wizened mummy. Her eyes were closed, though she had that vertical wrinkle in the middle of her forehead which usually meant she was annoyed. She looked as though her eyes would pop open at any moment and she would demand tea with extra sugar and cream.

After a long moment, Marc, ever the practical physician, asked what we should do. Jon did not answer him, and Tina just shook her head. Monique tried to speak, and stopped when the swordpoint pressed into her throat.

As for the rest of us, we knew it was hopeless. Vampires did not come back after being staked with wood. It was impossible—even those formidable night creatures had to follow their own rules. But none of us had the heart to let Marc and Jessica in on this fact. We were just using this time to begin to recover from the shock.

It had been, as the deaths of all charismatic individuals are, too sudden, too quick. We wanted time to grieve.

Jessica was straightening out Betsy's bangs,

which were quite disheveled, and I could see her tears dripping down on Betsy's still face.

"Oh, Bets, Bets . . . it's not fair. We figured it out. If we'd just been here a minute sooner . . . we could have saved you! We *should* have!"

She was young.

"I just can't do this again," Jessica wept. "I wasn't supposed to have to go through this anymore with you. You've got to stop dying on me!"

"Well, forget it," Marc said abruptly. He put his hand on the stake protruding between Betsy's breasts. Jon put out a hand to stop him, but Marc shook his head so hard, his own tears flew. "I can't stand to see her like this, you guys. Like a bug tacked to a fucking board. It's not right, and I'm not havin' it."

And, with a wrench and a grunt, he yanked the stake out of her chest.

Betsy's eyes flew open, which of course, startled everybody.

Chapter 27

I felt a sharp burning in my chest, heard my shirt tear, and opened my eyes to give whoever-it-was a piece of my mind.

"Owwww!" I complained. "Dammit, this is a new shirt!"

There was a *thump* as Sinclair dropped me. Why he'd been holding me I had no idea—his sneakiness and hidden agendas were boundless. "Elizabeth," he said, and I was startled to see his lips were dead white.

"Owwww again! What'd you do that for?" I rubbed the back of my head. "What are you guys all staring at? You're freaking me out." And they were! I was looking up at a moon of faces, and every one of them had their mouths hanging open. I was afraid if I stayed where I was, I'd get drooled on.

"Buh," Jon said.

"Yeah, okay. What happened? Where's that sneaky cow, Monique? Oooh, she's toast! Did you guys know she was the bad guy? She totally is! She tricked me into coming and partying with her. Except some party—she *staked* me in the chest. I mean, who *does* that? And it hurt like hell! And what took you guys so long? Why am I lying on this disgusting floor? Sinclair, help me off this floor right now."

"Buh," Jon said again. Not sure what the boy's problem was, but right now I had bigger fish to fry.

"You're alive!" Jessica blurted. "Again."

"Look at this hole in my shirt," I complained. "Does she think cotton grows on trees? Wait a minute. It does, doesn't it? Or does it grow on bushes? Either way, I . . . mmph!" I beat at Sinclair's shoulder until he stopped kissing me. "Dude! Time and place, okay? Now let me up."

He hauled me to my feet and Jon threw his arms around me, which made me stagger. Then Sinclair peeled him off me and started making that peculiar growling noise again, and Jon sort of bristled back, and Jessica snapped at them both to cut the shit, but I didn't care because I spotted Monique, who was backed up in a corner and had a sword at her throat, courtesy of my new best friend, Tina.

"Ha!" I said, yanking the stake away from Marc, who let out a yelp and then pulled a splinter out of his palm. "Stake *me* in the chest, willya? And you *ruined* my shirt."

I marched over to Monique, who managed to look

amazed, scared, and pissed, all at the same time. "False queen," she said defiantly as Tina stepped away. Made me sort of nervous. I kind of wished that the sword was still pointing at my nemesis *du jour*. "You'll never rule."

"Tsk, tsk. Someone skipped her Book of the Dead bible lessons. Apparently I *am* ruling. It's just, losers like you didn't get the memo."

"You're talking too much," she said. "You always do."

"Awww, that hurts, Monique! It gets me right here." I touched the gaping hole in my shirt. "Where's the love? Say, while I'm thinking about it, you dropped something over there." I hefted the stake. "I think I'll give it back. If you don't mind."

"You don't have the—*urk!*"

"Oh, gross!" Jessica cried, turning away.

"Sorry," I said, stepping back and surveying the staked Monique with—I admit it—not a little bit of satisfaction. "What can I say? Death is messy. And she had it coming." I tried not to sound as whiney and defensive as I felt.

Because she *did* have it coming. For what she made the Blade Warriors do to all those other poor vamps, never mind what she did to me. Let her explain herself to the devil, if she could. *I* didn't care.

"Nicely done," Sinclair commented. He was looking a little better—not so deathly pale (for him)—which was a relief. And he wasn't growling at Jon like a rabid bear anymore.

"I wanted to do it," Jon pouted.

"It was sort of my job," I explained. "You can kill the next evil vampire serial killer."

"Oh." He visibly perked up. "Okay. I'm glad you're not dead for real."

"Me, too," Marc and Jessica said in fervent unison.

"Yeah, um, what's up with that? Monique's not going to come back like I did if I take that stake out, is she?"

"Of course not," Tina said, sounding shocked. "No one ever does. I mean . . . besides you. No one has ever . . ." She trailed off and shook her head, looking mystified, which for someone that smart, was a pretty rare thing.

"And that's interesting, isn't it?" Sinclair asked.

"Interesting," Jessica said, still looking a little green around the gills, "is so *not* the adjective I'm thinking right now." She shook a finger under my nose. "You . . . you . . ." She didn't have to say any more. I could tell she had been through hell again.

He ignored her. "I don't believe the Book of the Dead mentioned just how . . . unkillable . . . Elizabeth seems to be."

"Well." I shrugged. "You know. Hard to keep a good woman down, and all that."

"Particularly now," he said dryly, "with all your new possessions."

"What?"

"By our law, when you kill one of us, their possessions become yours."

"No way. Really? What about their families?"

"Vampires don't have families," Tina explained patiently. "Except for you, apparently. Didn't you wonder why Nostro's house never sold? It's yours."

"Sweet! First Sarah's Armanis, now this! Did you see Monique's Porche? Mine, all mine!" I stopped, because Marc and Jessica were giving me funny looks. "I mean, not that I killed her just to get the car, or anything." That was just a sweet, sweet bonus.

"No," Tina said, giving me a funny look of her own, "but I think that's the story we'll spread."

"How come?"

"We'll have to," Sinclair said, "until you work up some ruthlessness. Otherwise, this problem will keep coming up. Others will assume you're an easy kill, and will try for your crown."

"Who cares? She's obviously unkillable."

"Nobody is," Father Markus objected. "Not even Christ."

"Besides, I'm plenty ruthless," I protested. "I killed two vampires this week! *And* I put the milk back last night when there was just a tiny bit left."

"That was you?" Marc asked.

"Although . . ." I nibbled my lower lip, thinking. "I didn't kill Mr. Mason, and I sure should have."

"Mason? Your supervisor at Macy's?"

"Yeah, he's Monique's evil minion! He totally set me up. Fired my ass, then tipped her off so she could scoop me up like a minnow in a bait shop. Jerk."

"Really." Sinclair's eyes went flat. "Elaborate." He made me tell him the whole story, and then he took me over it one more time. Everyone was appropriately outraged on my behalf. It was great!

"I can't believe your boss tried to kill you, too," Jessica said. "I mean, I know they're trying to keep the unemployment rate down, but that's ridiculous."

"Most people think their bosses are out to get them. But mine really was! Eh, never mind him . . . now what? I mean, besides changing my shirt. This is just"—I looked down at myself—"yech."

"We have much to discuss," Sinclair announced.

"You're right about that," Tina said, looking disturbingly fervid. "What does this mean? For all of us, and for our queen?"

"It will make for some fascinating additions to my papers," Father Markus admitted. He looked like he could hardly wait to sit down at a desk and write. Bo-ring.

"Majesty, you're with us again! Unprecedented! And—"

"Look, you two . . . I realize you can't help being total buzz kills, but we're not having any big panel discussion tonight. It's Friday, I've shrugged off death's clammy embrace—"

"Again," Ani said.

"—and I want to dance!"

"I could use a drink," Jessica admitted, "or five."

"Me, too," Marc chimed in. He wiped sweat off his forehead. He and Jessica still looked really rattled. "It's really stressful, watching you come back from the dead."

"I'm sorry," I said humbly. "It's been a bad week for everybody, I guess."

"No more of this getting killed crap," Jessica ordered.

"Hey, it's not exactly fun for me, either! It's not like I'm doing it for the attention." There was an annoying, pointed silence. "I'm not!"

"Where are you going dancing?" Ani asked.

"Nowhere you can get in," Jessica said shortly. "This is strictly a roommates-of-Betsy unwinding thing."

"I'm a roommate of Betsy," Sinclair said mildly.

"I guess we could go to Gator's," I said. Then the horrible words sunk in. *"What?"*

"Oh, did I not mention it?" He looked so innocent; butter wouldn't melt on his fangs. "We're leaving the Marquette; it's no longer adequate for our needs. And after some discussion of the problem earlier this evening, Jessica has kindly agreed to be our landlord."

"You're moving in?" I was going to faint. I was going to throw something. I was going to get new sheets. "You . . . I . . . you . . ."

Jessica spread her hands and shrugged. I shot her a murderous glare. All that "she's in love with him and she doesn't know it" talk I'd overheard! And she'd been planning *this*.

I never should have slept with him again. Jessica wouldn't have jumped to dumbass conclusions if she hadn't seen us in bed together. Oh, I knew it! I knew

I'd be sorry for that moment of weakness, but even I couldn't have foreseen this. *Nothing good comes of having sex with Eric Sinclair!*

I put a hand up, rubbed my forehead. "I really need that drink now."

"We're in a bar," Jon pointed out.

"Forget it, you little weirdos," I said rudely, including Ani in my diatribe. "A) I'm not partying in dead Monique's tacky club, and B) you guys aren't even drinking age. So you're not coming."

"Oh. Almost forgot." Jessica fished in her pocket, then stretched something shiny toward Eric and Tina. "Here's your house key."

I snatched it from her and ate it. I gagged, but it went down.

"Oh, very mature," Sinclair sniffed, but I could sense the smirk lurking.

"Don't talk to me." I paused, to see if the key was going to come back up. It was staying put, for now. "And *you* . . ." I grabbed Jessica's ear and she yelped. "Come on. I'm driving my new Porche somewhere and you're gonna explain yourself." After I threw up the key.

"It just makes fiscal sense . . . if you look at the numbers I'm sure you'll—let go!"

"He can sleep in my room," Marc offered.

"I suppose I should say something negative about vampires living in sin," Father Markus said, "but that seems to be the least of your problems."

"Actually, I've already picked out the room next to Elizabeth's—do not attempt to grab my ear," he added quickly as I twitched in his direction. "Unless you wish to be put across my knee."

"Oh, is that what you guys are up to when the sun goes down?" Ani teased, as Jon reddened and looked away.

I got out of there, dragging Jessica and Marc, before my head exploded.

Epilogue

So now I'm living with stupid Sinclair and stupid Tina in a gigantic mansion that I can't afford. *And* I'm undead and unemployed. Again.

Okay, well, Tina's not so stupid. In fact, I kind of like her when she's not startling me with her core of utter ruthlessness. Plus, she makes a mean strawberry smoothie. Even Sinclair drinks them! I guess he really loves strawberries. I gotta change my shampoo.

Strange vampires keep dropping by to show tribute. Apparently Monique's little coup failure has been making the gossip channels, because dead people are falling all over themselves to stop by and say howdy. For some reason, they bring blood oranges. Sinclair says it's tradition. I say it's cracked. The fridge is full of the damned things.

I thought Marc and Jessica were nuts to open their—our—home to more vampires, but Marc earnestly explained that he doesn't think of Tina and Eric as undead. I bet he'd change his mind if either one of them ever got hungry enough.

As for Jessica, she's made up her mind that as long as Sinclair and I are meant to be, we might as well start getting used to each other. And it'd be rude to leave Tina out, since she and Eric are practically brother and sister. Thus, we are now roommates. I searched her room, but could find no evidence of drug use.

It's unbelievably nerve-wracking to come downstairs and find Sinclair already in the tea room, reading the *Wall Street Journal* and getting a smirk ready.

Not to mention, I've been fighting the almost constant temptation to sneak into his room wearing nothing but a smirk of my own. But I realized my lesson in Monique's club: nothing good can come of having sex with Eric Sinclair. And as for the gentleman in question, he's been . . . well, a perfect gentleman. Dammit.

He and Tina brought the Book of the Dead to the house, where we keep it in the library on its own little mahogany book stand. Jessica tried to read it and got a three day migraine for her pains. She also jumped at small noises and wouldn't eat for most of those three days. Now she stays the hell away from the library.

I'll get to the book myself someday, but for now I'm trying lighter fare. Let Tina and Sinclair manage the thing, if they could.

When I rose a few nights ago, there was a copy of

Pat Conroy's biography, *My Losing Season,* on my chest. It took me a week to read it and the best part was, there was no mention of food anywhere. So I put it on the shelf with my other books. Guess a door I thought was closed had swung open again . . . I was sure glad.

I tried to thank Sinclair (I knew Jess hadn't done it; she'd have made sure she got the credit . . . but I bet she gave him the idea), but he gave me a look like he didn't know what I was talking about, so I dropped it.

Jon left town. He said he wanted to get back to the suburbs to see his family, but I think, and Jessica concurs, he couldn't stand the thought of Sinclair living with me. Which made two of us, frankly. He promised to come back at the end of the summer, and I actually find myself missing the little weirdo.

Ani hangs around most evenings. I think she and Tina have something going, but they're discreet. Still, they're both doing a lot of wandering around the mansion, humming. And the goofy smiles are annoying.

Sinclair was right: Monique's stuff came to me. It was true. She really did have several properties all over the world. And *two* cars!

What the hell I was going to do with a club in Minneapolis, a spa in Switzerland, a private school in England, and a restaurant in France remains beyond me. I don't know a damn thing about managing multiple businesses. I guess I could go get a job at one of them. Maybe I'd try to run Scratch . . .

Detective Nick Berry's peripheral involvement in the whole nasty business was that rarest of things. A true coincidence. The cabbie I'd saved had just happened to give his report to Nick. Nick had just happened to see my car a few days later and pulled me over. I was glad. I'd messed up his life once before; I would have hated to find it a ruin again.

Mr. Mason disappeared. I didn't even know about it until I saw the blurb in the paper. He had no family, and his own boss was the one who finally reported him missing; how's that for sad?

Gone without a trace, until they found a few pieces of him in his apartment a month later. Inside a suitcase, which he'd apparently been in the middle of packing when . . . when whatever happened, happened. I asked Sinclair about it, and he just turned the page of the *Journal* and didn't answer me. So I didn't bring it up again. Felt a little sorry for Mr. Mason, though. After all, he *did* give me a job at Macy's.

Went to see the Ant, with a Calvin Klein onesie for my future half-sibling. Sort of a "can't we pretend we don't hate each other?" ice breaker. She "accidentally" spilled red wine on it.

I'm worried about the gardener. Nobody else talks about him, and when I describe him I get a lot of funny looks. Jessica says she did hire someone to take care of the lawn and flowerbeds, but it was a young woman in her twenties. This guy's old, really old.

I'm pretty sure I'm the only one who can see him.

I'm scared to go talk to him, but one of these days I plan to get it over with. Whatever his deal is, hopefully I can help, and he'll vamoose like Marie did. I miss *her,* but creepy old guy ghosts staring up at my bedroom window whenever I look out I do *not* need.

I did a lot of thinking about what happened that night in Monique's bar. The whole day—week!—had a fairly nightmarish quality and sometimes it's hard to remember all the gory details. Whenever I try, my mind veers off to sweater sales and leather gloves. All the winter stuff is in the stores now, and I need to stock up.

Jessica asked me about it, and Tina did, too, but Sinclair avoided the subject entirely, and I wasn't sure why. I told them the truth—I didn't remember much between getting staked, and Marc pulling the stake out.

What I didn't tell them was the one thing I *did* remember: Sinclair's voice floating out of the dark, coaxing, commanding, and saying the same thing over and over again: "Come back. Come back. Don't leave me. Come back."

Weird. And sometimes I wonder if I dreamed it. Or hallucinated it. Or, most amazing of all, if he really said it. God knows I wasn't going to ask him . . . I was still building up my courage to talk to the dead gardener.

So, either I can't be killed, or the king of the undead brought me back by the sheer force of his will. Either way, something to think about.

But not today. Neiman's is having a sale, and I

desperately need a cashmere cardigan. I'd prefer red, but I'll take any primary color. Jessica's paying! She says it's a "congrats on coming back from the dead again" present.

Works for me.

Author's Note

PRETTY much without exception, the events in this book are entirely made up. Vampires don't stay at the Marquette Hotel; nor do they work the cash registers at Macy's.

However, as of the time of this writing, if you go to a WorkForce Center in Minnesota, they aren't allowed to answer questions about unemployment insurance. And at some centers, you really aren't allowed to use their phones to call someone who can. Honest.

Also, visitors to Summit Avenue will note that the house across from the governor's mansion A) isn't Betsy's, and B) isn't at the end of the block. Artistic license, which is a fancy way of saying I was lazy.

CONTINUE READING FOR A SPECIAL PREVIEW OF MARYJANICE DAVIDSON'S NEXT NOVEL

Derik's Bane

COMING SOON FROM BERKLEY SENSATION!

The present

MICHAEL Wyndham stepped out of his bedroom, walked down the hall, and saw his best friend, Derik Gardner, on the main floor headed for the front door. He grabbed the banister and vaulted, dropped fifteen feet, and landed with a solid thud he felt all the way through his knees. "Hey, Derik!" he called cheerfully. "Wait a sec!"

From his bedroom he heard his wife mutter, "I *hate* when he does that . . . gives me a flippin' heart attack every time," and he couldn't help grinning. Wyndham Manor had been his home all his life, and the only time he walked up or down those stairs was when he was carrying his daughter, Lara. He didn't know how ordinary humans could stand walking around in their fragile little shells. He'd tried to talk to his wife about this on a few occasions, but her eyes always went flinty and her gun hand flexed, then the phrase "hairy fascist bastard" came up and things got awkward. Werewolves were tough, incredibly tough, but compared to Homo sapiens, who wasn't?

It was a ridiculously perfect day outside, and he couldn't blame Derik for wanting to head out as quickly as possible. Still, there was something troubling his old friend, and Michael was determined to get to the bottom of it.

"Hold up," Michael said, reaching for Derik's shoulder. "I want to—"

"I don't care what you want," Derik replied without turning. He grabbed Michael's hand and flung it away so sharply Michael lost his balance for a second. "I'm going out."

Michael tried to laugh it off, ignoring the way the hairs on the back of his neck tried to stand up. "Touchy! Hey, I just want to—"

"I'm going *out*!" Derik moved, cat quick, then Michael was flying through the air with the greatest of ease, only to slam into the door to the coat closet hard enough to splinter it down the middle.

Michael lay on his back a moment like a stunned beetle. Then he flipped to his feet, ignoring the slashing pain down his back. "My friend," he said, "you are so right. Except you're going out on the tip of my boot. Pardon me while I kick your ass." This in a tone of mild banter, but Michael was crossing the room in swift strides, barely noticing as his friend Moira, who had just come in from the kitchen, squeaked and jumped out of the way.

Best friend or no, nobody—*nobody*—knocked the alpha male around in his own. Damned. House. The other Pack members lived there by his grace and favor, thanks very much, and while the forty-room house had more than enough space for them all, certain things were simply. Not. Done.

"Don't start with me," Derik warned. The morning sunlight was slanting through the skylight, shining so brightly it looked like Derik's hair was about to burst into flames. His friend's mouth—usually relaxed in a wiseass grin—was a tight slash. His grass-green eyes were narrow. He looked—Michael had trouble believing it—ugly and dangerous. Rogue. "Just stay off."

"You started it, at the risk of sounding junior high, and you're going to show throat and apologize, or you'll be counting your broken ribs all the way to the emergency room."

"Come near me again and we'll see who's counting ribs."

"Derik. Last chance."

"Cut it out!" It was Moira, shrieking from a safe distance. "Don't do this in his own house, you idiot! He won't stand down and you two morons—schmucks—losers will hurt each other!"

"Shut up," Derik said to the woman he (usually) lovingly regarded as a sister. "And get lost . . . this isn't for you."

"I'm getting the hose," she warned, "and then *you* can pay to have the floors re-sealed."

"Moira, out," Michael said without looking around. She was a fiercely intelligent female werewolf who could knock over an elm if she needed to, but no match for two males squaring off. The day was headed down the shit hole already; he wouldn't see Moira hurt on top of it. "And Derik, she's right, let's take this outside—*oooof*!"

He didn't duck, though he could see the blow coming. He should have ducked, but . . . he still couldn't believe what was happening. His best friend—Mr. Nice Guy himself!—was challenging his authority. Derik, always the one to jolly people out of a fight. Derik, who had Michael's back in every fight, who had saved his wife's life, who loved Lara like she was his own.

The blow—hard enough to shatter an ordinary man's jaw—knocked him back a full three steps. And that was that. Allowances had been made, but now the gloves were off. Moira was still shrieking, and he could sense other people filling the room, but it faded to an unimportant drone.

Derik gave up trying for the door and slowly turned. It was like watching an evil moon come over the horizon. He glared, full in the face: a dead-on challenge for dominance. Michael grabbed for his throat, Derik blocked, they grappled. A red cloud of rage swam across Michael's vision; he didn't see his boyhood friend, he saw a rival. A challenger.

Derik wasn't giving an inch, was shoving back just as hard, warning growls ripping from his throat, growls which only fed Michael's rage

(rival! rival for your mate, your cub! show throat or die!)

made him yearn to twist Derik's head off, made him want to pound, tear, hurt—

Suddenly, startlingly, a small form was between them. Was shoving, hard. Sheer surprise broke them apart.

"Daddy! Quit it!" Lara stood between them, arms akimbo. "Just . . . don't do that!"

His daughter was standing protectively in front of Derik. Not that Derik cared, or even noticed; his gaze was locked on Michael's: hot and uncompromising.

Jeannie, frozen at the foot of the stairs, let out a yelp and lunged toward her daughter, but Moira moved with the speed of an adder and flung her arms around the taller woman. This earned her a bellow of rage. "Moira, what the hell? Let go!"

"You can't interfere" was the small blonde's quiet reply. "None of us can." Although Jeannie was quite a bit taller and heavier, the smaller woman had no trouble holding Jeannie back. Jeannie was the alpha female, but human—the first human alpha the Pack had known in three hundred years. Moira would follow almost any command Jeannie might make . . . but wouldn't let the woman endanger herself or interfere with Pack law that was as old as the family of Man.

Oblivious to the drama on the stairs, Derik started forward again but Lara planted her feet. "Quit it, Derik!" She swung her small foot into Derik's shin, which he barely noticed. "And Daddy, you quit, too. Leave him alone. He's just sad and feeling stuck. He doesn't want to hurt you."

Michael ignored her. He was glaring at his rival and reaching for Derik again, when his daughter's voice cut through the tension like a laser scalpel. "I said *leave him alone!*"

That got his attention; he looked down at her in a hurry. He expected tears, red-faced anger, but Lara's face was, if anything, too pale. Her eyes were huge, so light brown they were nearly gold. Her dark hair was pulled back in two curly pigtails.

He realized anew how tall she was for her age, and how she was her mother's daughter. And her father's. Her gaze was direct, adult. And not a little disconcerting.

"What?" Shock nearly made him stammer. Behind him, nobody moved. It seemed nobody even breathed. And Derik was standing down, backing off, heading for the door. Michael, in light of these highly interesting new events, let him go. He employed his best Annoyed Daddy tone. "*What* did you say, Lara?"

She didn't flinch. "You heard me. But you won't hear me say it again."

He was furious, appalled. This wasn't— He had to— She couldn't— But pride was rising, blotting out the fury. Oh, his Lara! Intelligent, gorgeous—

and utterly without fear! Would he have ever *dared* face down his father?

It occurred to him that the future Pack leader was giving him an order. Now what to do about it?

A long silence passed, much longer in retrospect. This would be a moment his daughter would remember if she lived to be a thousand. He could break her . . . or he could start training a born leader.

He bowed stiffly. He didn't show the back of his neck; it was the polite bow to an equal. "A wiser head has prevailed. Thank you, Lara." He turned on his heel and walked toward the stairs, catching Jeannie's hand on the way up, leaving the others behind. Moira had released her grip on his wife and was staring, open-mouthed, at Lara. They were all staring. He didn't think it had ever been so quiet in the main hall.

Michael was intent on reaching his bedroom where he could think about all that had just happened and gain his wife's counsel. He didn't quite dare go after Derik just yet—best to take time for their blood to cool. Christ! It wasn't even eight o'clock in the morning!

"Mikey—what—cripes—"

And Lara. His daughter, who jumped between two werewolves with their blood up. Who faced him down and demanded he leave off. His daughter, defending her dearest friend. His daughter, who had just turned four. They had known she was ferociously intelligent, but to have such a strong sense of what was right and what was—

Jeannie cut through his thoughts with a typically wry understatement. "This *can't* be good. But I'm sure you can explain it to me. Use hand puppets. And me without my So You Married A Werewolf guide . . ."

Then he was closing their bedroom door and thinking about his place in the Pack, and his daughter's, and how he hoped he wouldn't have to kill his best friend before the sun set.

Revenge is a dish best served cold.
—Pierre Choderlos de Laclos (1782),
Les Liaisons Dangereuses (*Dangerous Liaisons*)

WHEN Pietra Lang's granddaddy had an affair, it was infidelity. But when her grandmother found out, it became murder. . . .

Or so Eugenié's chicken bones said.

Pietra, better known as Pete to her friends, might have grown up accepting the Cajun housekeeper's mysticism, but a message about an old murder was a doozy to pull out from the great beyond, even for Eugenié Thibodeaux. Pete squinted at the mangled chicken carcass scattered on the kitchen's wooden cutting board, trying to divine more than good soup stock. She failed.

"Bones don't lie," Eugenié said.

Maybe they do.

The uncertainty niggled at Pete.

Eugenié's foresight was usually half a bubble out of plumb but seldom entirely off beam, like the summer the bones told her Pete would meet up with someone tall, dark, and good-looking. She did. He turned out to be a horse.

At any other time, Pete would've jogged upstairs and pried the straight scoop from her grandmother. That wasn't possible now though, since the old gal had died yesterday. She had been a woman steeped in potent Southern roots, emotional, unpredictable, touched with charisma, and given to histrionic flourishes. Not much about her antics could surprise Pete anymore.

Still . . .

"And this murder'll be revealed when?" Pete asked the housekeeper.

Eugenié shrugged and scraped the chicken pieces into a steaming pot, the multicolored glass bracelets on her wrists tinkling an exotic rhythm. Her funeral-white turban and caftan made her dark eyes intense and fathomless within her smooth brown face.

She might have been fifty or eighty, Pete couldn't say. She'd worked for the family for thirty years and never seemed to age.

"Bones don't tell when, missy, just what."

That could mean five minutes or fifteen years from now, so Pete quashed her curiosity and planted her feet squarely on the temporal plane.

"My schedule's packed," she said around a mouthful of warm buttermilk biscuit. "What with the family coming in, the Fourth of July committee giving me fits, and burying Grandmother, there's no way I can squeeze in a scandal or anything else right now. No time."

"Everything has a time," Eugenié said, nodding. "You'll see." Then she made a shooing motion with her hand. "Now, scat! I got me plenty of hungry people to feed . . . and haul them catfish outta my kitchen."

Pete shoved away from the granite countertop, telling herself not to be ridiculous. She neither put stock in the housekeeper's predictions nor ignored them.

But murder?

Then again, given all the wrinkles in the Lang family, she had good reason to feel a nagging sense of unease.

Homicide in a prominent Southern family was definitely juicy news, the stuff of prime-time sudsers. And watershed scandals were nothing new to the Langs.

They had made their money the old-fashioned way—they inherited it—and that was a strike against them in the media, for no matter how justified an act might be, wealth equaled power and, to some people, guilt.

Temperatures neared ninety-five degrees and climbing in Langstown, a small town nestled in the panhandle. Live oaks. Southern Baptists. Quiet money.

Outside, the air was thick and stifling. Barely any breeze moved through the red, white, and blue bunting that festooned the upper balcony railings of Grandmother's home in celebration of the upcoming holiday.

The one-hundred-twenty-year-old antebellum house was Pete's pride, her first project in Langstown to be restored to the grandeur and romance of the Old South. At that moment, seventy-five of the town's most influential were enjoying her handiwork as they milled about deep in the shade of the wide verandas or beat the summer heat in the air-conditioning that billowed starched organdy curtains through the opened French doors.

They had dropped in to pay their respects as much as to rhapsodize over Eugenié's homemade beignets served with café au lait. Later, there would be barbecue ribs, ham, Cajun slaw, macaroni salad, and enough cakes, cookies, and pies to induce insulin shock served on banquet tables spread with red-checkered tablecloths under the shade of the towering oaks. So it was a sure bet no one was leaving short of an earthquake.

Pete had slipped into an unadorned black cotton sheath dress to play hostess, a role she'd relinquish to her mother, Racine, once her private plane landed from Los Angeles. A devotee of Our Lady of Accessories, Racine lived to hobnob.

She also believed in marrying well and often, a philosophy subscribed to by her older daughter, Phoebe, but one not shared by her younger daughter. Her greatest regret was that Pete had yet to land herself a captain of industry.

The year Pete turned thirty, Racine finally accepted that her younger daughter loved working in historical restoration and would likely never leave the sleepy rural community. That same year Racine revised her matrimonial hopes for Pete down to simply a man with a pulse.

Once Pete had greeted the mourning visitors, she roped her long-time friend Albert into helping her lug the cooler full of heavily iced catfish filets down to the old boathouse where Grandmother's fish freezer sat. The July Fourth committee, which Pete chaired, planned a catfish fry as part of the town's annual Independence Day activities, but Eugenié needed the fridge space in the house for the extra guests.

Albert was both a curiosity and a fixture in Langstown. He lived in Tallahassee but often made the ninety-minute drive to play escort whenever Pete represented the family at a county fund-raiser or a historical society function.

The two of them got along so well because they were kindred spirits. Down through the years, they'd both subjected themselves to blind dates, even when they knew the inevitable outcome would still be two people looking for something other than what they'd found.

Today, he wore his usual Hawaiian print shirt and Sperry Top-Siders with no socks but had opted for dark cargo shorts and a black armband as concessions to her grandmother's recent passing. They crossed the manicured carpet grass and down the winding crushed oyster-shell pathway, Albert struggling with his end of the heavy cooler, thanks to a two-pack-a-day habit, while Pete led the way.

Three of her grandmother's dogs tagged alongside, on the lookout in case one of the pond mallards ever decided to launch a frontal attack. She'd named the mutts after her favorite all-female group, the Andrews Sisters.

A walker/yellow Lab mix was the alpha, while the ancestry of the other two was in doubt beyond a bit of terrier, a lot of dark fur, and a shared fondness for shredding lacy underwear. Pete had learned to like Jockey thigh-highs in self-defense.

Behind them, the whir of car tires crunching over the gravel driveway mixed in with muffled voices, the metallic slam of car doors, and the constant whine of crickets. A pair of squawking mockingbirds strafed a blackbird that was too close to their nest, and a hound dog bayed somewhere off in the woods, probably scenting a deer. The mouthwatering aroma of smoked ribs saturated the air.

"Good God," Albert wheezed, sweating freely. "Whose idea was this? I'm in no shape for manual labor."

"C'mon, couch potato, just a little farther."

"I prefer divan diva, if you don't mind." And on that note, Albert stubbed his toe on a protruding shell but quickly recovered. "Jeez, I think I dropped my 'nads back there."

"Don't worry about it," Pete said, trudging on through a swarm of no-see-ums. "You don't use them anyway."

"Like you can talk. I know nuns who see more action."

"Don't go there, you sound like my mother."

"At least I'm looking. You? You're doing nothing but biding time with that beanpole mortician."

The sun beat on Pete's face and melted her makeup. She could feel it sliding down her cheeks. Gauging by the sticky feeling under her arms, her deodorant wasn't putting up much of a fight either.

"Vonnie Miller's a nice man," she said. "Safe."

"Safe is the last thing a man wants to be called, unless it's being said at his parole hearing. Trust me, toots. Keep looking. You can do better. The right man is out there just waiting for you to find him."

How often had Pete heard that? Too many to count. Racine quoted the trite saying like scripture, especially around the holidays.

"So how come I have to do all the looking?" Pete said. "Why can't he look for me for a change?"

"Fat chance of him finding you here in the boondocks."

About then, the plastic handle slipped out of Albert's sweaty grasp. He swore and jumped to save his toes as his end of the cooler slapped the ground with a grating screech, forcing Pete to either drag the cooler or stop. She stopped.

One of the blue-haired guests yoo-hooed to Pete from the upper veranda and waved. She shaded her eyes, recognized Mrs. Conroy, one of her grandmother's friends from the Eastern Star, and returned the wave.

"What's the old bag barking about?" Albert asked.

"I have no idea," Pete said, nodding and smiling as if she understood the woman's every word. "Probably another pitch for her grandson, the air-traffic controller from Memphis."

"Good-looking guy?"

"A salad bar of neuroses."

"Never mind then," Albert said. "But while we're on my favorite topic . . . spill your guts about Danny Benedict. Have you seen him yet? Is he as gorgeous as his pictures? I want all the details."

"Yes, yes, and he's not your type."

Albert deflated.

While he consoled himself with a smoke, Pete slid the black scrunchie off her wrist and bunched her brown hair at the back of her head to lift it off her damp neck. The humidity had turned her new 'do into a mass of frizz.

She debated how much to share with Albert.

He knew Benedict was a high-powered divorce lawyer. They'd seen pictures of him in *People* magazine, usually with some celeb's ex-wife stuck to his side like a hair on a biscuit. But Albert didn't know Benedict had come to meet with Pete's older brother, Jackson.

Jackson intended to ditch his wife of ten years so he could marry his podiatrist. Since he was up for reelection to the state legislature in November, he understandably decided it was more politic to keep this business low profile.

The problem was that Albert and Jackson disliked each other, had done so from day one. Whenever they were in the same room, it was like watching two dogs square off in the middle of a junkyard. So, as much as Pete adored Albert, low profile meant not sharing that tidbit with him.

Thinking back on meeting Benedict at the hospital, she recalled casually elegant clothes, an expensive shirt and creased slacks, smoky brown eyes, and a sensuous mouth; the kind of man her grandmother would say could walk into a room and tame women like snakes.

"Benedict's okay," Pete said, "if you like the tall, blond, and devastating sort."

Albert snorted. "It would be tough, but I could force myself to get used to it."

"I'm sure his dog loves him, too."

Another puff and Albert flipped his cigarette into the boxwood bushes, so Pete hefted her cooler handle and continued toward the boathouse.

"The man didn't have to come to the hospital," she added, more to herself than to Albert, "but he did. He's okay."

Out of her league was more like it. She was a plain, ordinary woman with plain, ordinary tastes. From what Pete had read about Benedict in the gossip sheets, she was no match for a man who kept a string of glamorous women and waltzed through them faster than kudzu through the backyard.

Up ahead of her, the boathouse overlooked a spring-fed lake that had been stocked years ago with large-mouthed bass, bream, shellcracker, and bluegill. Pete never cared for fishing, but as a kid, she used to come down to watch the wood ducks fly in at dusk to nest in the reedy wetlands on the far edge.

Now as she approached, a hungry bass exploded on an unsuspecting frog that snoozed close to the seawall. The surface of the murky water churned foamy white for a second then quieted into gentle ripples.

The building itself was a rustic, gloomy catchall outbuilding, seldom used since Granddaddy Lang had passed away the decade before, except by mud daubers and doves that homesteaded the opened rafters. In his day, it was rumored, the boathouse was often the scene of stolen kisses and illicit rendezvous with women of abandoned character who seemed intent on picking the gold out of his teeth.

The design was utilitarian—Pete's favorite euphemism for functional and butt ugly. Apparently, Grandmother had liked it that way, since she had refused to include the outbuilding during the restoration of the big house.

Pete never understood why. Too many memories, perhaps. Now that the old gal was beyond fussing, Pete made a mental note to spruce up the facade to give it more character, more integrity with its surroundings.

She unlocked the metal door and stepped gingerly past spiders and grinch-green tree frogs waging a turf war over the clutter of sprinkler parts and rusty fishing lures that littered the warped wooden shelves. The place smelled old and musty, like the inside of an unwashed running shoe.

"Ye gods and little fishes," she said, "when do you suppose was the last time this place was cleaned out?"

"We'll herd the livestock later," Albert wheezed with an impatient hand wave. "Open the freezer, toots. Chop, chop. I'm dying here."

"You sound like an old fud."

"Knowing you has made me an old fud."

"Yeah, yeah, the wailing wall is around back."

Then Pete turned and yanked open the ancient upright freezer and stopped short.

"Oh, my aching . . ."

Her mouth worked, but no more words came out.

She slammed the door shut as quickly as she'd opened it, then swallowed hard.

"What now?" Albert griped.

"Did you have a good breakfast?" Pete said after a moment.

"Grits and eggs, my usual. Why?"

"You may be seeing it again."

Then, afraid to look, afraid to confirm what she'd seen, Pete inched the door open until it swung wide on its hinges.

And there it sat, her worst nightmare and Eugenié's damned chicken bones in the flesh.

Of everything that could be leftover in her grandmother's freezer, the last thing Pete expected to see was the barefooted bleached-blonde who was defrosting inside.